Blood Alley
A. S. Fleischman

Introduction by
David Laurence Wilson

Black Gat Books • Eureka California

BLOOD ALLEY

Published by Black Gat Books
A division of Stark House Press
1315 H Street
Eureka, CA 95501, USA
griffinskye3@sbcglobal.net
www.starkhousepress.com

BLOOD ALLEY
Originally published by Gold Medal Books, New York, and
copyright © 1955 by A. S. Fleischman

Reprinted by permission from the estate of Sid Fleischman. All
rights reserved under International and Pan-American
Copyright Conventions.

"Sid Fleischman and the Biggest Trick of All" copyright © 2022
by David Laurence Wilson

ISBN: 978-1-951473-84-6

Cover design by Jeff Vorzimmer, ¡caliente!design, Austin, Texas
Book design by Mark Shepard, shepgraphics.com
Proofreading by Bill Kelly
Cover art by Alfredo Capitani from the Italian movie poster

PUBLISHER'S NOTE:
This is a work of fiction. Names, characters, places and
incidents are either the products of the author's imagination or
used fictionally, and any resemblance to actual persons, living
or dead, events or locales, is entirely coincidental.
Without limiting the rights under copyright reserved above, no
part of this publication may be reproduced, stored, or
introduced into a retrieval system or transmitted in any form
or by any means (electronic, mechanical, photocopying,
recording or otherwise) without the prior written permission of
both the copyright owner and the above publisher of the book.

First Stark House Press/Black Gat Edition: August 2022

"There's never a dull moment when Fleischman is at the helm."
—*Publishers Weekly*

"[Fleischman] specialized in the 'one damn thing after another' school of fiction… don't try to keep up; just let the story wash over you and have a good time."
—Michael Scott Cain, *Rambles*

"Fans of Gold Medal novels will know him best as the author of the fast-moving, cinematic paperback thrillers with which he began his career."
—Bill Crider

"Fleischman can write his tail off…"
—*Paperback Warrior*

BLOOD ALLEY

"…good adventure fiction in a pulp vein."
—David Vineyard, *Mystery*File*

"…an admixture of suspense, fireworks and romance kept bubbling at a slow boil."
—*New York Times*

had a career with two themes, magic and fiction. Fibs.

Fleischman fell in love with stage magic in the fifth grade. In 1935 he joined the San Diego Magician's Club and a year later he was performing with a friend as "The Mirthful Conjurers." Later he played nightclubs and traveled with a spook show during the last gasps of vaudeville.

Magic was a profession, a life-long avocation, and the theme and setting of many of Fleischman's stories. His style was "close-up" magic—simplicity and dexterity—including the manipulation of cards and matchbooks—seemingly common, low-key objects that could astonish and tricks that could be shared.

He wrote his first book of magic tricks, *Between Cocktails*, in 1939, his last year of high school, when he was still too young to drink a beer.

Fleischman never performed escapes, no holding of breath or slipping out of manacles, but he was encouraged by Harry Houdini's widow. In his autobiography, *The Abracadabra Kid*, he shares a mid-thirties photo of the two of them standing in Balboa Park. He is watching her eagerly. It looks like Mrs. Houdini is holding a deck of cards.

When Sid created a new trick, or, more often—a variation on a classic—he would publish these new secrets in publications intended for magicians and sometimes he'd sell the "secrets" by mail. Magic paid his tuition for his first two years at San Diego State College. Between 1942 and 1947 he published four more books of tricks with the artist and magician Bob Gunther.

Ultimately Fleischmann's best and biggest magical trick was a vanishing act—to make an entire Chinese village, 180 people, their tools, goats and shrines—disappear. That was the story of *Blood Alley*.

Sid Fleischman and the Biggest Trick of All

By David Laurence Wilson

Albert Sidney Fleischman, who wrote as both A. S. Fleischman and Sid Fleischman, was a gentle, thoughtful and soft-spoken man who had a notably long and eclectic career, publishing in nine decades. In the nineteen fifties he was a successful writer of western, detective, international crime and intrigue. He was a noir writer and a writer of screenplays. And he wrote some of the most entertaining how-to books that have ever seen print.

Then he became a beloved, award-winning author of books for children and young adults and he never stopped, publishing into his ninetieth year, albeit posthumously.

Sid was born in 1920, a Brooklyn native who grew up in San Diego, California, a city blessed by natural beauty and Balboa Park, the site of the 1915 Panama-California exposition and the 1935-36 California Pacific International Exposition. Another benefit was a fabulous main library with a good selection of books on magic and occultism and later—books on the study of flying saucers.

You see, for Fleischman, it all began with magic. Like the crime writers Walter Gibson (*The Shadow*) and Clayton Rawson (*The Great Merlini*), Fleischman

In 1941, while still a student at San Diego State, Fleischman joined the Naval reserve. Two days after the bombing of Pearl Harbor he was called up for active duty. He avoided basic training when the Navy found he was a proficient typist but when he shipped out, he was aware of his deficiencies.

Later, he wrote: *"I wonder if I am the only sailor who ever went to war unsure which side of the ship was port and which was starboard."*

Fleischman married Betty Taylor in 1942 before shipping out to Borneo, the Philippines and China. He was in the Navy until 1946. After his discharge he spent more than a year writing, submitting, and accumulating rejections for his short stories. Fleischman returned to San Diego State to receive a degree in English in 1949. For a time, he worked as a journalist in San Diego.

A lot of crime fiction writers were in and out of San Diego during the thirties and forties and Fleischman, Oakley Hall (who wrote his mysteries as Jason Manor) and Bob Wade and Bill Miller (who teamed as "Wade Miller" and later, as "Whit Masterson"), all attended San Diego State at the same time. After graduation they began to populate the town with their own fictional detectives.

Fleischman entered the field with an entry level job: two novels for Phoenix Press featuring the private detective Max Brindle, *The Straw Donkey Case* (1948) and *Murder's No Accident* (1949). That was Fleischman's best shot at a career based on volume. The results were unsatisfactory, the reward meager.

The two Max Brindle novels represented a young writer's experiment and were written in a manner that did not come comfortably to Fleischman. He wrote them, in essence, to simply try and get his name on a published novel. He'd read somewhere that a writer should be able to finish as many as 20 pages a day and both he and the books suffered as he wrote as speedily as possible to try and match that challenge.

Sid was a different kind of writer. He found later that for him, his natural pace worked best, a careful, painstaking attempt to select the very best words for every sentence and sentences that were simple but clever. He was a versatile, fastidious writer who was not only satisfied but often quite pleased when he produced one page of finished fiction during a day of work. He liked to start his days with a clean, blank sheet of paper.

Slow and steady, he once described his process as carving novels out of marble. He didn't want or need a mountain of words, he simply sought out the best words. He relied more on erosion than speed as he'd "chip away" at a book.

□ □ □

I was surprised and delighted when I learned that Stark House intended to publish a new edition of *Blood Alley*, Fleischman's best-known adult novel and curiously, the last of them to be reprinted. With this publication all of Fleischmann's paperbacks for adults are in print and available from Stark House, including *The Sun Worshippers*, a posthumous original published in 2016.

The first time I met Sid was in 1976 when I was studying the films of director William Wellman for a collection of essays. Fleischman had begun working with Wellman in 1954.

I had already spoken to Wellman's screen-writing collaborators Niven Busch (COLLEGE COACH, 1933), Robert Carson and Robert Pirosh

(BATTLEGROUND, 1949). Carson had worked on several films with the director, including A STAR IS BORN (1937), NOTHING SACRED (1937), BEAU GESTE (1939) and THE LIGHT THAT FAILED (1939).

In contrast to the veterans, Fleischman seemed a surprisingly young man. He was a pleasant acquaintance, agreeably introspective, accessible and forthcoming, though by 1976 he had already left the field of suspense to become a writer of children books. He was still married to Betty, a union that would remain until her death in 1993. They had three children.

Sid did not dismiss the novels of A. S. Fleischman—that young writer from the nineteen fifties——rather, he seemed to enjoy their resurrection, so he cheerfully discussed characters and contracts, machetes and conflicts set in a Far East of decades past.

◻ ◻ ◻

A big step for the novelist came in 1951, when *Shanghai Flame* was published in Fawcett Publications' Gold Medal series. The Gold Medal books featured action, suspense and adventure and they were geographically democratic. Fawcett was as willing to feature a murder in the jungle, swamp, or desert, as they were to stick to urban streets. Fleischman's novels were set in China, Bali, Macao and the British colony that would become Malaysia. What Fleischman didn't know personally he convincingly researched.

The novels were hard work. If he could write two books a year he was on a good pace. "Actually, when I get to about 220, 240 pages, I'm glad to see the end," Fleischman said.

□ □ □

In 1954 Fleischman was living in Carmel, California when he finished *Blood Alley* and submitted it to Fawcett.

Fleischman's protagonist was Capt. Tom Wilder, a thirty-one year old, resourceful but alienated skipper who has spent a year imprisoned by the communist government of China.

"Except for his ship and his crew, Wilder had come to feel no responsibility for the world he lived in," Fleischman wrote. *"He didn't care to distinguish himself. He was indifferent to the opinions of others ... He'd finally taken a square look at the world and found it crooked. He decided not to change it."*

This time magic gets in the way of action, as fortune-telling stones are tossed and the zodiac and *feng shui* are used to define the best time to dispose of a body. Wilder is a skeptic.

□ □ □

Fawcett's editor, Dick Carroll, was a friend of Robert Fellows, a partner with actor John Wayne in the motion picture production company Batjac. He arranged for Batjac to see a copy of the new manuscript.

A week later Fleischman received a call from Batjac. The company wanted to purchase the film rights for the book before publication. They offered $5,000. It was enough, Fleischman figured, to support his family for a year.

Days later he heard from William Wellman, the accomplished and notorious film director, World War One Flyer and Hollywood Bad Boy with a body of work matched by few. Wellman had recently directed two aviation films for Batjac, ISLAND IN THE SKY

(1953) and THE HIGH AND THE MIGHTY (1954), both starring Wayne. Wellman was going to direct BLOOD ALLEY. He wanted Fleischman to write the screenplay.

Wellman and his producers thought the book was cinematic, so much so that they had a strong suspicion that it might be a pseudonymous book written by one of the Hollywood Ten, blacklisted screenwriters suspected of communist leanings. That unlikely suspicion could have made the deal go sour.

Even more unusual was the fact that Fleischman had never even seen a screenplay before he began writing one for BLOOD ALLEY. He was suddenly the sole writer on a two million dollar motion picture.

After Fleischman finished the script in Carmel, Wellman asked him to begin work on a screenplay for his next film, GOODBYE MY LADY, adapted from the novel by James Street. Fleischman purchased a home in Santa Monica, where he would live for the next fifty years.

Wellman liked to collaborate with his writers and he liked to keep them available for sudden, intuitive revisions. He expected a script to evolve. Wellman was 59, over twenty-five years older than the neophyte Fleischman.

Over the next weeks they went over the book and the script page by page and Wellman was uncharacteristically patient. They met three or four times every week, and spoke by phone daily.

With Fleischman, Wellman was trying to recreate the "chemistry" of his extended collaboration with screenwriter Robert Carson.

Fleischman recalled this unexpected turn in his career: "Wellman had an uncanny eye. To begin with, he was a great gambler with talent. A man in his position, with all the great films he made, he should have been working with major, best-selling novels. But he wasn't that kind of man. He liked to throw the dice and take a chance."

For six or seven weeks Fleischman shuttled between Santa Monica and Sausalito, where the BLOOD ALLEY production—including stars Robert Mitchum and Lauren Bacall—was headquartered.

The company purchased a sternwheeler riverboat and used it for a week of location hunting on the Sacramento River. Along with Wellman and Fleischman, the party included assistant director Andrew McLaglen and Art Director Alfred Ybarra.

During the voyage they came across a graveyard of ships, a collection of old beached boats. "It had nothing to do with our story, but Bill got terribly excited," Fleischman recalled. "It's a gift," Wellman said. "It would cost us half a million to build a set like this!" Fleischman recalled some resentment over having to rework his story to fit that scene.

On the first day of shooting Mitchum knocked the film's Head Driver off a gangplank and into the chilly waters of San Francisco Bay. He was fired and sent home and Wayne took over as Wilder without missing a beat. The production went ahead with the script as written. Wayne was 47, ten years older than Mitchum and idealistic but surly. He expresses himself in the film by talking to an imaginary friend he refers to as "Baby." Undoubtedly Mitchum's performance would have been less heroic, more cynical, and it might have produced an altogether different film.

Another revision was necessary when Capt. Wilder was supposed to conceal the ferry by throwing nearly all its supply of food and grains on the decks and smokestack to attract a camouflaging covering of seagulls. The production purchased all the day-old sourdough in San Francisco, scattered it over the deck of the ferry boat and waited for the birds to arrive.

At the same time, however, there was a heavy herring run off the coast and apparently the gulls preferred fresh fish to day-old-bread. The ferry boat only attracted about 50 gulls. The major scene was thrown out and Fleischman had to make more adjustments to the script.

BLOOD ALLEY was a disappointment at the box office. In the long run it would be regarded as a broadly-painted anti-communist fable. Fleischman didn't think that either he or Wellman was trying to produce an anti-Red movie, but that the Chinese setting was simply a good one for an adventure story.

The wide-screen Cinemascope photography, at times, was spectacular.

Fleischman was reconciled to accepting credit for the script, a first effort and an embarrassment, he said, that he had to watch "every ten seconds, it seems, on a television screen."

As far as his work in movies, Fleischman said, "it paid the rent."

The original paperback novel was released in conjunction with the film and featured a cover painting of Wayne and Bacall. Below that, white print on a red background urged: "Read it — and see why we had to make this great novel into a motion picture — JOHN WAYNE" An episode of the popular television series "I Love Lucy" also featured Wayne promoting BLOOD ALLEY.

□ □ □

GOODBYE MY LADY (1956), originally titled as THE BOY AND THE LAUGHING DOG, had the distinction of offering Walter Brennan his favorite role. In a sly piece of foreshadowing, the Daughters of the American Revolution gave it their award for the best children's picture of the year.

After GOODBYE MY LADY Batjac cut its costs by laying off most of its staff. Wellman stayed on at Warner Brothers, where he would work on DARBY'S RANGERS (1958), and then on another dream project, LAFAYETTE ESCADRILLE (1958), which harkened back to Wellman's own World War One experiences.

For Fleischman, who received sole screenplay credit, LAFAYETTE ESCADRILLE, based on Wellman's experiences during World War One was a difficult, frustrating effort. They didn't have enough money or the right kind of actors, he said.

Wellman tried to generate another Hollywood story with Fleischman, a sequel of sorts, to A STAR IS BORN. There were other efforts that didn't catch on. For Wellman it was the end. He never made another film.

□ □ □

Fleischman wrote seven paperbacks for Gold Medal and another one for Ace. In 1963 the last of his suspense novels, *The Venetian Blonde*, was set in Venice, California, with nary a Chinese or Malaysian accent to be heard. In *The Venetian Blonde* Fleischman's hero can identify the manufacturer of a playing card from the way the card feels in his hand. Undoubtedly Fleischman had the same talent.

Now he was ready for another metamorphosis. He began writing a story for his children, turning from the sex and violence of his suspense novels to draw upon his early background as a touring magician. He invented "Mr. Mysterious," a frontier magician who outwits both outlaws and warlike Native Americans. He named his characters after his children and read each chapter to them, soliciting their opinions.

Though he hadn't written the book for publication,

he sent it to his agent, along with a note of apology. *Mr. Mysterious & Company* was purchased overnight by the Atlantic Monthly Press. Fleischman entered the world of juvenile fiction and there he would remain. He would now be writing for kids. Historical fiction became his specialty.

□ □ □

By the time we spoke in 1976 Fleischman was a different man, though his magic, in every sense of the word, remained.

There was still conflict, and loss, within his writing, but now his writings were infused with hope and themes of overcoming obstacles. He was no longer the formidable sounding "A.S. Fleischman" who wrote of deception, war, death and other human foibles. Now he was Sid, a personable, talented and lucky man.

He became an eminent writer of stories for children, international and inter-generational books that were translated into nineteen languages.

In 1987 he received a Newbery Medal for *The Whipping Boy*. In 1996 he wrote a fine autobiography and topped it off with biographies of Harry Houdini, Mark Twain and Charlie Chaplin. As we enjoy his early career we must also honor the writer he became, the lucky magician who produced sixty-five books out of thin air.

—May 2022
Portland, OR

David Laurence Wilson has contributed to Stark House editions of the crime fiction writers W. R. Burnett, Arnold Hano, Day Keene, Wade Miller, Harry Whittington and William R. Cox. He is also working on an illustrated history of American daredevils and stuntmen.

Blood Alley
A. S. Fleischman

Chapter One

He set fire to his mattress a few minutes after ten that night.

He straightened, a gaunt figure in cotton trousers, and watched the flames chew along the ticking. Sleep had settled over the jail like a reprieve. Wilder stood back calmly. It was done. Wait a moment longer.

He could hear the two guards at the end of the corridor gossiping in their harsh Fukien accents. The turtle of a ferryboat from the Chinese mainland had broken down again, causing Black Pigeon to be late for his shift. And if the typhoon struck, Black Pigeon would be marooned on this ink spot of an island. Wilder tried not to think about the typhoon.

The straw blazed. Flames sucked up the old mattress and colored Wilder's bearded face. Smoke began to boil out into the corridor. He squared his shoulders and walked to the bars of his cell.

"Fire! *Huo!* Guards! *Huo! Huo!*"

The guards came on the run, lapsed into confusion, and shouted commands to each other. With their baggy mustard trousers tucked into canvas shoes, they looked to Wilder like buffoons.

Finally they carried in buckets of water and Wilder stood by, ignoring the sputtering contempt they hurled at him.

Twenty minutes later the guard known as Black Pigeon waddled into the cell with another mattress.

The machinery of Wilder's escape was under way.

He certainly hadn't believed a word of it. In more than a year of Red jails, and a commonplace career before that as a China skipper, Tom Wilder had developed a taste for the ridiculous. An escape plan, literally delivered to him on a platter, was absurd.

The note had come smuggled in the red rice he'd had for breakfast.

He'd read it, grinned a little, and gone on eating.

The Reds, of course, had planted the note themselves. It amused him to think that the damned thing had probably been done in triplicate with copies to the proper commissars. He could see them rubbing their hands expectantly in their main-floor offices. Let the American dog intoxicate himself with the wine of escape, and then cork the bottle.

He'd rejected the gift of *hsi-nao-chin*—brain washing. He'd confessed nothing. He'd signed nothing. But they were still trying to break him down, this time with a greasy wad of paper. They'd got his ship and he supposed they would, in time, get his mind. But not today, gentlemen.

He'd detached a steamed cockroach from his rice and finished breakfast.

But as the day wore on, Wilder had kept returning to the note. The instructions were absurd, of course, but just supposing for a minute that the Reds hadn't sent it—who had? He doubted that Hong Kong had been able to trace him to Kulangsu Island in the Amoy port area. The Reds had moved him around so much during the first few months that he doubted if even they knew quite where he was.

By noon he'd decided he'd be a fool not to try. Even if the whole business were merely designed as a People's comedy, he'd be prepared to shrug it off. And if they were letting him out on a string only to jerk him back again, he might see a chance to keep running.

It was a temptation.

He'd try.

He stood now scratching through his beard, damp

from the night's oppressive heat. The smell of wet ashes lingered in the cell, and for several minutes Wilder did nothing but wait for the guards to settle down. He kept glancing at the new mattress—unmistakably lumpy. With his chiseled nose and tufted black eyebrows he'd taken on the extravagant look of a pirate. The beard, he reminded himself, would have to go. It would make him a preposterous sight on the hilly streets of Kulangsu. He hadn't shaved since Hong Kong; they'd taken his razor.

Finally he walked to the bunk and started a rip in the mattress ticking.

He worked quickly now. He could hear the guards at the end of the corridor once again worrying each other over the limp typhoon flags hung from the signal-tower yardarms. Wilder tuned them out. He knew he would have to beat the storm or be trapped on Kulangsu by high waters. He'd worry about that later.

He got a hand inside the mattress, explored with his fingers, and a moment later pulled a well-polished Russian half boot out of the rice straw. He saw at once it was going to be too short for him. He found a straight razor. A pair of dark-blue trousers with robin's-egg piping down the sides. The other black boot.

And he found a gun.

He stopped.

A grin cracked his chapped lips. For the first time there was a spark of emotion in Wilder's deep-set eyes. The gun was real.

The escape was real.

The touch of cold metal was electric. The Reds wouldn't be crazy enough to put a gun in his hand. Wilder's sturdy aloofness deserted him. His mind breezed to Hong Kong and freedom, more than three hundred miles to the south. It seemed, suddenly, incredibly close.

He examined the gun quickly. Russian. A Tokarev service pistol. He released the magazine and checked the load. Eight beautiful steel bullets.

He stuck the gun in the waistband of his trousers and returned to the mattress. A cap with blue piping and a bright red star. He found no identification papers to go on, and only a little currency. When he unfolded the gray-green jacket with its silver epaulets, crossed pick and shovel, and triangle of silver stars, he realized he was to make his escape in the uniform of a senior lieutenant of engineers in the Russian army.

He hacked his beard down to a stubble and shaved without a mirror. The limp typhoon flags fluttered in his mind. He dressed. The coat was binding at the armpits and the stiff collar was tight as hell. The boots were a squeeze; later, he'd throw them away. He fixed the cap square on his head and wished he could stop sweating. His face had a crazy, airy feel without the beard. He could no longer keep his hopes battened down. He was, he admitted to himself, excited as hell.

In five more minutes he ought to be walking down the hill outside his window.

The mattress. Black Pigeon had obviously been bribed, Wilder thought quickly. The note. The evidence was to go. He didn't take time to wonder again who had planned it all, who in this Red port gave a damn about an American on an island in the harbor.

For the second time he set a mattress fire.

The comedy repeated itself with the same props. The water buckets came, the baggy pants, the copybook abuse. But once the guards entered the cell, Wilder stepped from behind the bunk and the flames lit up the Tokarev.

Black Pigeon put on a quick, boastful front; the other gaped at a beardless Wilder as if some demon had come to life in a Soviet uniform.

"*K'uai k'uai!*" Wilder said. "Put down your buckets and face the wall."

He sapped them quickly, doused the fire, and locked them in the cell. He assumed Black Pigeon had expected to be struck and let it go at that.

He walked stiff-backed to the steel fence at the end of the corridor. Black Pigeon had left the gate unlocked. Sweet, venal Black Pigeon. Wilder took a deep breath and went down the flight of stairs, seeing no one. He strode past the administration offices, shut for the night. He heard the night voices of a dozen clocks on a dozen walls. The hall was deserted.

It can't be this easy, he thought suddenly. Once again suspicion gripped his mind. Was he being watched? He envisaged smiling brown eyes behind the dark transoms. Was it, after all, going to be a farce?

His boots rang along the stone floor.

He turned a corner and saw a guard, sweating under the weight of his bandoliers, stationed at the entry doors. Wilder's heart began to pound. Ten yards. Five. Beyond stood the open courtyard and the night.

A sleepy salute. A muttered "*Man-tzow.*" The open sesame of his Soviet uniform. The smell of garlic breath as he passed.

The night.

The sampan wasn't there. He walked to the end of the jetty, his eyes searching the shadowy waters along the piles. All right, there's a hitch, he told himself. Wait out the sampan.

The boots were hell, his contact was nowhere in sight, but he couldn't stand still. He was in the first wild flush of escape and had to keep moving.

He'd clipped along the streets of the former international settlement, seeing almost no one. Part way down the hill there'd been a pair of off-duty soldiers loitering near the walls of the U.S. Consulate, now contemptuously plastered with Red posters. He'd passed along the other side of the street and kept a smart stride all the way to the harbor. The island seemed hunched, like a man holding onto his hat, waiting for the typhoon to hit.

Now he'd walked to the end of his instructions—Sankoochan jetty. "A sampan loaded with bean-cake fertilizer will be waiting for you among the others...."

He grimaced. He doubted if there was a sampan left in the harbor. Any other night they'd be all over the place, but tonight was different. The typhoon was an absurdity and Wilder cursed it under his breath. As well as he could remember, it was April, and that was too early in the year for a typhoon. Take it up with the nearest commissar.

He spread his legs and stared resentfully at the lights of Amoy Island, across the harbor. The old tea port raised its bulky granite shoulders against the night sky. Somewhere off to his left, a couple of miles away, stood the Chinese mainland. Where was that smelly sampan?

He thought about taking off the boots. The uniform was suffocating and he mopped his face. No sampan coolie was going to risk the harbor with a typhoon tracking toward the coast. Whoever had planned his escape hadn't planned on the wind. Sankoochan jetty looked like it would be a waste of time.

He had no time to waste, but he refused to give it up. Maybe he was ahead of schedule. He'd wait a little longer. Nothing stirred but the outgoing tide, swirling around the piles under his boots. The lights of Amoy had never seemed closer, and the oyster beds, uncovered by the tide, had never smelled so fresh.

Wilder felt, for a moment, as if he were the last man

left on earth.

To hell with the sampan.

He turned sharply and started back toward the dock. His eyes shot past the godown roofs, up the hill, to the jail. Its night lights flickered in the heat. He hoped never to look at the place again. He made up his mind that wherever he spent the night, it wasn't going to be on Kulangsu Island. He'd known it in the sleepy days before the Reds, when the Amoy taipans and consuls lived there, but he'd had enough of Kulangsu to last for the rest of his life.

It had been a sharp humiliation to lose his ship ten miles outside of Hong Kong. He had been within sight of Dragon's Back that night when the Red gunboat had come out of nowhere and a little pock-marked Chinese had taken over the bridge. The rest was a bad dream. But he had dreamed too of grabbing his pound of Red flesh in return. He would blow up a bridge. He would sink one of the People's ships. He would leave his size-eleven footprint somewhere and return the humiliation in kind. It was entirely a personal matter, he felt, between Tom Wilder and Red China.

The dockside came closer, and he dreaded it a little. Which way should he turn? He refused to consider that there might be no way off the island. He checked the sky. How far at sea was the typhoon now? Cirrus clouds had ridden in with the hot spell and they stretched overhead like a taut embroidery.

Tonight, he thought bitterly, nothing could have smelled as sweet as bean-cake fertilizer.

Forget it.

Almost at the foot of the jetty, he stopped short. What had Black Pigeon said? The ferry had broken down and made him late.

The ferry. Wilder whirled and glanced off to his left.

The ferry slip was down there, several blocks away, at the foot of the Jardine and Matheson godowns.

He hurried. He remembered watching from his cell window as the stern-wheeler came limping in from the mainland. The harbor had since emptied, but nowhere in his memory had the ferry gone thrashing *out* again.

She was still in the slip—she had to be. They must be working frantically to get her repaired and out of the harbor, he thought. If the typhoon caught her in the slip, she'd be thrashed into driftwood.

All right, he'd be on it.

Wilder ran.

And time ran out on him. A steamy little whistle pierced the stillness and echoed through the dockside godowns. He had gone less than a hundred yards.

Wilder unbuttoned his coat and swore.

A moment later the steamer came thrashing into sight with a tail of foam. He watched it move into the stream and dig in, filling the night with the thumping of its paddle wheel. The last boat out of Kulangsu. Smoke and sparks boiled up from its stack, smudging the oppressive sky. It would dash for the river and hole up behind the mainland cliffs.

Wilder stared. The little gingerbread steamer was running for her life, and he couldn't tear his eyes away. It was lit up like something in a feverish dream. He could see a deck hand coiling a bowline. Along the saloon, stained-glass windows threw out colored fans of light, incredibly bright in the empty harbor. The stern wheel churned up a white bustle of spray. At the bow, tadpole eyes skimmed the water, staring sullenly toward the mainland.

Wilder shoved back his cap and got going again. Above him on the hills an occasional light flickered in the heat. Tomorrow, he knew, every *t'ung-chih* in the garrison would be out beating the island bushes for him. He cursed the typhoon, he swore at the ferry, but he refused to consider himself as hopelessly walled up on the island as he had been in jail.

His boots creaked. Bits of rice straw from the mattress still clung to his coat and a numbing year of prison routine clung to his mind. He seemed, for a moment, unable to think for himself, and fell into an aimless, bewildered stride. He kept looking at the sky and he kept squaring his shoulders, like a man fighting sleep, but he was fighting off panic.

The ferry whistle piped out short, outraged puffs of sound, and Wilder glanced toward the harbor again. He saw the steamer churning past the Butterfield and Swire wharf on the Amoy side, and he saw a flat shape caught in its lights.

A sampan.

The ferry beat down on it, the whistle screaming now, and Wilder began to run. The sampan coolie stood clearly outlined on his stern platform, his legs spread, his hands together, the long oar zigzagging in the notch of the sampan's split tail.

The ferry passed and the sampan was still there, rocking in the wake of the paddle wheel.

Wilder reached the tip of Sankoochan jetty and a moment later the sampan barked up against the piles. The odor of bean-cake fertilizer came with it.

"You're a sweet-smelling bastard." Wilder grinned and climbed down to the bow. "Let's get the hell out."

Chapter Two

Wilder first saw the village in the sprawling light of dawn. He sat under the sampan canopy, his boots upright beside him, the muddy coat thrown over his shoulders. He listened to the creaking rhythm of the oar and realized that the nose of the boat was coming around.

"Is that where we're heading?"

"It's my village."

Wilder glanced up the wall of the bluff. The village stood at a tilt, gripping the cliffside as if to keep itself from sliding off into the river below. An ancient crenelated stone wall ran crookedly around it, and a sturdy pine tree grew out of the remnants of a broken watchtower. The mountains behind came down in a pine-clad arm, leaped the river, and continued south.

"How is your village called?"

"Chiku Shan."

Wilder grinned inwardly. He was doing great. They were the first answers he'd been able to get out of the coolie. Less than a mile from Kulangsu he'd beached the sampan on one of the craggy little islands in the mouth of the river, and Wilder had helped him drag the boat up on the mud flats. A clap of wind caught them as they weighted it with boulders, and then the typhoon tracked in off the Strait and the sky vanished.

They had tried climbing to shelter in the abandoned pagoda above the cliffs, but the wind tore them from their footholds, and they had sat out the storm huddled among the rocks. Wilder had taken off his boots, and for almost three hours he didn't move a muscle. Loose tiles flew off the pagoda roof and sailed down in deadly arcs. He had been able to hear the close ones shatter like clay pigeons on the rocks.

The storm had only sideswiped the area. When it had passed, Wilder emptied the water out of his boots and turned a grin on the coolie. "Let's find your illustrious three planks and get going."

They had taken the north fork of the river, and Wilder fell into an even, patient mood. He'd been born an old China hand, and now he felt like the last of the breed around. Although he had a grab bag of Chinese dialects, the coolie had pretended not to understand his questions, and finally Wilder had let it go.

The coolie now rattled a pair of bamboo clackers and the sounds broke the river stillness. A signal, Wilder thought. He looked up, but could see no one at the walls. The place looked austere and medieval. He'd never heard of the village of Chiku Shan, but someone up there apparently knew of him. He'd have the answers soon enough.

They rounded the bluff and the coolie nosed the sampan into a tributary stream. Wilder wasn't prepared for what he saw; in the uncertain light he felt as if they were entering a sudden, hidden canyon.

The stream opened into a lagoon with sheer walls. A moment later Wilder had seen enough to wonder if he'd ever imagined any tucked-in corner of China as beautiful and peaceful. Three small fishing junks stood together at a stone landing, their lugsails furled. Behind the lagoon a waterfall plunged down the granite embankment and drummed in the brightening dawn.

He heard voices and then he saw figures hurrying down a narrow stairway carved in the hillside from the walls of Chiku Shan to the lagoon landing. The welcoming committee, Wilder thought. He pulled on his boots.

He saw three Chinese waiting at the landing when the sampan pulled in. They beamed, and, in the Chinese way, each man shook his own hands warmly in greeting, and Wilder stepped ashore.

"Welcome to our humble village, eminent brother."

While two of the men were straight-backed Fukien types, handsome in their old age, it was the big Chinese with the look of North China in his size that spoke. He had broad wrists and the feet of a Tartar; he carried his age with a certain rawboned nobility. Under the impeccable gray fedora his face was the color of tobacco, and long wrinkles shot from the heavy corners of his eyes, surrounding his smile. He was obviously the *ti-pao*, the village headman, and just as obviously he had put on his best silk gown for the occasion. In the fashion of old men with chin beards, he wore a comb on a silk ribbon around his neck. Fiddling with it, he introduced the village elders who flanked him.

"My humble name is Tso Ta-Tan."

Wilder shook his own hands firmly. He liked Mr. Tso on sight, but he detected a great air of expectation about the three of them, and it bothered him a little. A dog barked somewhere on the steps leading to the village, and Mr. Tso turned.

"Ah." He smiled warmly. "Miss Grainger comes to welcome the honorable captain. Good. Quite good."

Wilder saw a girl in a sweater and a tartan skirt on her way toward the landing; the dog pulled her along. Wilder tried not to stare, but he found it impossible not to. She was blonde. Wilder hadn't seen a light-haired woman since Hong Kong. Miss Grainger, he thought as she came closer, was almost worth waiting for.

She couldn't have been more than twenty, and he saw at once that she had the special stamp of an English girl brought up in China. It was there in the way she held her shoulders and a certain leisure in the way she walked. She was long-legged and wore sandals. He felt like a fool for noticing that she didn't fill out the sweater very well. As she came nearer he saw that her eyes were deep blue, with a certain willfulness about them, and her hair, ash blonde, was carefully parted to one side.

She reached the landing and stopped to pat the dog, as if overcome by shyness at meeting strangers. "This is Koxinga," she said, a little too quickly. "He's named after a pirate that used to live here."

"How do you do, Miss Grainger?" Wilder said with a stiffness that surprised him. He felt suddenly ridiculous, standing there in a mud-spattered uniform that was too small for him.

Mr. Tso formalized the introduction. "We trust your evening was without wayward incident." He smiled with an obvious taste for irony.

"It was a bit drafty," Wilder replied. Miss Grainger's cheeks were flushed from the long flight of steps and her nostrils flared slightly. She has quite a pretty nose, he thought, thin and faintly arched, and her hair looks as if she's been brushing it for hours.

"We apologize for the irascible wind," Mr. Tso said. "The night for your journey was selected by our *suan-ming-ti*. Come, food and sleep are waiting for you."

Wilder knew he'd have to sit through tea and small talk before Mr. Tso got around to the point of the whole affair. But if he was curious before, he was bewildered now. The elders obviously expected something from him.

They started single file up the worn granite stairway. Miss Grainger led the way, and behind him Wilder heard the elders chattering in their own dialect. Everyone, including the dog, an Irish terrier, seemed in a brisk humor. It gave Wilder a mild jolt that the night for his escape had been cast by the village oracle. The guy needed a barometer among his divining tools. Still, Wilder had made it safely to Chiku Shan, and he supposed that would save face for the *suan-ming-ti*.

"Do you live here in the village?" Wilder asked.

Miss Grainger glanced back and gave him an easy

smile. "Yes. It's lovely here. You'll like it."

"Am I staying long?"

"None of us are. Did I spell your name right?"

"What?"

"I wrote the note."

"Yes." Wilder smiled. "You spelled my name right, Miss Grainger."

"I don't suppose Chiku Shan would fall into the river if you called me Cathy."

"Cathy."

"You must be desperate to get out of that horrid uniform. We had no idea you were such a tall man, but perhaps my father's clothes will fit you a little better. He's been called away. He's a doctor."

"What am I doing here?"

"You're what Mr. Tso calls one of God's footsteps."

"Does that explain anything?"

"No," she laughed. "But Mr. Tso will."

"That," he said grinning, "I figured out for myself."

Of the short walk through the village, rooted on terraces with crooked cobbled paths connected to each other by weed-grown stairways, Wilder remembered very little. The only earth he saw was in flowerpots. The rest was stone and tile and plaster. What remained in his mind was a vintage Rolls-Royce standing on its rims in the courtyard of a two-story whitewashed house. He saw it as they passed the open gate. It seemed preposterous on a streetless village and Wilder wondered how they had got it up the cliffside. The brightwork gleamed and it was obviously fussed over by someone.

"The local taxi?" Wilder grinned.

"The skeleton in the village closet, Captain Wilder," Cathy answered with a cold shrug.

"I don't suppose," Wilder said, "Chiku Shan would fall into the river if you called me Tom."

"Tom."

A room had been fixed up for Wilder in Dr. Grainger's house, and Cathy's amah, a dumpy little woman with beautiful brown eyes, led him upstairs to change. It was a plastered room with an antique brass bed, polished to a golden sheen, a fireplace, and shuttered windows that looked down on the glazed tile rooftops of the village, the muddy river, and the pine hills beyond.

Wilder felt the mattress. It seemed impossibly soft. He sat on the edge of the bed, trying to collect his thoughts, and it seemed to him suddenly that he was in the grip of something entirely unreal. Kulangsu couldn't be more than eight miles away, and yet he had somehow been whisked into a different world. He felt in no danger, and yet the houses, the river, and the hills outside the shutters were still Red China. What did the elders of Chiku Shan want with him? His escape, it appeared, was a village project, and he could see no sense to it. If he were discovered, every person in the village would be stoned before a People's court. And Cathy. This room. Clean clothes laid out on the bed. He shook his head. Cathy seemed incredible against the harsh stone of the village. Why hadn't Dr. Grainger got her out of Red China years ago?

Wilder noticed a hand mirror on the pine chest and decided to see what he looked like after a year on the wrong side of China. The reflection brought a grimace to his lips. He had never considered himself handsome, but there had always been a jaunty humor in his black eyes, a way of looking at the world, and now it was gone. A diet of red rice, fish soup, and pickled cabbage had cost him some weight and brought out the square boniness of his face. He had shaved badly in his cell the night before and decided to give it another try. He sure as hell needed a haircut and his skin needed some sun. The face he saw was like an apparition. He examined his teeth and tried a smile. He felt like a damned fool and put the mirror aside.

He cleaned up and tried on the straw sandals that had been left for him. They were a better fit than the boots. He was buttoning the white shirt when the amah knocked at the door and told him breakfast was ready.

"Ah," said Mr. Tso when Wilder came down. "I see that Captain Wilder has deserted the Russian army."

"I hope permanently."

"We will return the lieutenant's uniform to the cleaning shop in Amoy from which it was—borrowed."

"What about the gun?"

"That came from another source. You may keep it."

They ate in the high-ceilinged dining room, the windows open to the breeze, Cathy, Wilder, and the three elders. It wasn't until tea had been served and the amah sent away that the small talk passed and Mr. Tso got around to what was on everyone's mind.

"We had expected an older man," he said frankly.

"I'm thirty-one."

"No matter." His eyes narrowed and the deep lines in his face set. "You are experienced along the China coast, Captain Wilder?"

Wilder put down his tea and saw that Cathy was staring at him like the others. He felt suddenly as if he were on trial, and his patience deserted him.

"What's this all about?"

"The village put up the bribe money for your escape," Cathy put in evenly. "Black Pigeon was expensive. I think the village is entitled to find out what it has to know about you."

"If I reach Hong Kong I'll return the money."

"That won't be necessary," Mr. Tso protested briskly. "Your presence in Kulangsu was one of God's footsteps.

So. Quite so. We are honored by your presence in Chiku Shan."

"How did you know about me?"

"It was gossiped that an American sea captain was on the island. We investigated and found it to be true."

"All right," Wilder said. "I've made the run from Hong Kong to Shanghai thirty or forty times. I think I know the coast."

"Could you take a ship through the Strait to Hong Kong without maps?"

"I don't know," Wilder said. "I've never tried it."

"It is a difficult coast, is it not?"

"I'd say it would be very risky without charts. It's rocky all the way and there are hundreds of submerged dangers—including wrecks of ships that had charts."

"Still, you have navigated these dangers many times."

"Yes."

"It could be done?"

"With luck."

"I see."

"Mr. Tso is trying to say," Cathy said, "that we haven't been able to steal any charts."

"Captain Wilder," the *ti-pao* continued, picking up the comb hung around his broad neck and stroking his wispy comma of a beard, "you will have the choice of rejecting our unworthy proposition and traveling your own way to freedom. So. Quite so. But in that event we must request the utmost secrecy beyond these village walls. One unguarded word and our one hundred and eighty lives would be forfeited."

"You have my confidence, at least," Wilder said uncomfortably.

"Ah, yes. Thank you."

Mr. Tso's fingers opened and the comb dropped on

its ribbon. The room fell quite still and Wilder realized that with the old man's next words he would be drawn within some sort of village conspiracy. He disliked confidences and felt somehow tricked. He could feel Cathy's eyes on him, taking his measure, and then his resentment turned into a brittle sort of amusement. Whatever this plan of theirs, he hoped it wasn't so foolish that he'd have to turn it down.

"Our people," Mr. Tso said with a certain repressed anger in his voice, "can no longer live in peace under the hawks and dogs that now sit in Peiping. Our savings have been squeezed from us. One of our families has been uprooted to slave on the northern desert. Who will be next? Teaching one warns a hundred. Yes. We are warned that our children will grow up to be hawks and dogs like the rest."

"I see."

"Our people have chosen to leave Chiku Shan."

"The entire village?"

"We intend to leave nothing but the bare walls of our homes. Does the idea startle you?"

"I suppose it does."

"We will take everything—the tools of our trades, our animals, our shrines."

"Where to?"

"We will voyage to Hong Kong."

"You don't have charts. Do you have a ship?"

Mr. Tso folded his parchment fingers and leaned slightly forward. His broad face shone. Somewhere in the village Wilder heard the laughter of children. "In the tradition of our ancestors, we will acquire a ship, now that we have its captain. Our ancestors were patriots—and pirates."

Wilder remained unmoved. They were going to steal a ship. "It's been done before."

"Exactly."

Wilder was impressed with the audacity of the plan, and it made a swift appeal to him, even though he refused to show it. There would be a fine retribution in cracking through the bamboo curtain with a stolen ship. But maybe it was only black smoke out of an opium pipe, and he didn't allow himself to be caught up in Mr. Tso's persuasive emotions.

Cathy's eyes turned a burning resentment on him, as if secretly enraged at his stoic face. "Months of planning have gone into this. Every detail. It's going to work."

"Have you picked out your ship?"

"Of course."

"With the harbor patrol boat you might stand a chance of fighting your way down the coast."

"For many reasons," Mr. Tso cut in softly, "there is but one ship suitable for our voyage. We will take possession tomorrow night, if you agree."

"I suppose," Wilder said, "the time for this piracy has been determined by your geomancer."

"Quite so," Mr. Tso replied, sensing Wilder's low regard. "He is gifted in such things."

"What ship?"

"The one that travels the river to Amoy. The *ming-lün-ch'uan*."

Wilder's calmness deserted him. "The paddle-wheel ferry?"

"Exactly."

He knew his face had flushed. Audacity had turned to madness. These people were dreaming. He'd better put them straight before they killed themselves. The little stern-wheeler was the last ship on the coast fit for the dash to Hong Kong.

Chapter Three

He glanced at their faces, embarrassed suddenly by the disappointment in their eyes as they read his own expression. He took a deep breath and decided he'd better get on with it.

"The ferry's a relic," he said softly. "It must be sixty years old, maybe more. I've watched it come and go in the harbor. When it's not broken down, I doubt if it can make six knots."

"Eight," Cathy said quickly.

Their eyes met, and Wilder couldn't ignore the flash of hostility he saw. "Eight. Assuming we cleared the harbor, the patrol boat would overtake us before we lost sight of Pagoda Point."

"The patrol boat," Mr. Tso said, "will be taken proper care of."

"I see. Have you considered that there will be other gunboats in the other harbors south of here?"

"We are prepared for necessary risks. By traveling only at night, we expect to avoid attention."

"I'm to navigate at *night* without charts?"

"Quite so."

Wilder realized there was no point in laboring the subject. "My guess is the ferry draws about ten inches—maybe not even that. That's fine for your rivers, but Formosa Strait gets very rough, and if I'm not mistaken this is April and the rainy season, despite yesterday's weird hot spell and the pipsqueak of a typhoon. We may catch some bad weather before we see Hong Kong and I doubt that the ferry can take much of a sea."

"It is a solid ship, built in your own illustrious country," Mr. Tso said, and Wilder had the feeling he was only making a fool of himself. His statements carried no impact, as if these objections had been thoroughly thrashed out long before he appeared on the scene and the village decision made in the face of the unique risks involved.

"All right, that's all I have to say," Wilder said hopelessly.

"Captain Wilder," Mr. Tso began, matching up his fingertips, "had you not seen these objections we would think you a fool and would hesitate to put our humble lives in your hands. Clearly, you are not a fool, and I think we shall succeed. Consider, please, that because the boat is so shallow we can hide ourselves among the rocks and the streams of the coast. The month of April also contains fogs to make us invisible. And because we go in such an unseaworthy boat, the wine-drinking comrades will surely look for us to cross the Strait to Formosa itself—one third the distance. Instead, we will go south to Hong Kong. Is all this not so?"

As the old man spoke, his voice crisp and sure, Wilder felt somehow that his own remarks had been cowardly. It was clear that the elders were going to try this mass escape, and they were determined to make it on an absurd little ferry. He saw now that nothing he said could make any difference. If he refused to master their ship, they would wait patiently for another China skipper to wash up on the Amoy shore.

"It is not necessary for you to make your decision at once," Mr. Tso said. "If you have no taste for our adventure, we will understand, and you will be free to go your own way."

"I'd like a few hours to think it out," Wilder said seriously. The village had arranged his escape and it would be impossible to shrug off a sense of obligation. But at that moment he was doubting his own seamanship. How much, after all, did he remember of the coast?

"As you wish."

The three elders rose, bowing toward Cathy, their smiles betraying nothing of their anxieties. But at the door Mr. Tso turned, and Wilder was again impressed by his size.

"Captain Wilder, it is to be expected that a search for you will be made in the village. I must warn you that one of our families is—unreliable."

"Communist?"

"So. Quite so. Today all the Fengs attend a family funeral in Changchow on the south river. Until their return you have the freedom of our village walls."

"I understand."

"We expect them home tomorrow." He hesitated. "Yes. Once they return, you must keep within this house. They prefer not to visit Dr. Grainger, and you will be safe from them. I regret this inconvenience. It is unfortunate."

The three elders left, moving silently down the steps in their silk slippers. There was the scent of cold tea at the table. Cathy hadn't moved.

"He's too big for South China," Wilder said. "Like someone left over from the old Manchu conquest."

Cathy's eyes were blue and terribly cold. Whatever shyness she had felt at the lagoon landing was no longer apparent. "You're not going to do it, are you?"

"I didn't say that."

"But you won't do it. You think it's utterly mad, don't you?"

"Yes."

"We're going to try it anyway."

"I can see that."

She tossed back her hair. "I'm not sure I like you, Captain Wilder."

"You were going to call me Tom."

"I've changed my mind."

Wilder smiled faintly. There was spirit to her, something untamed inside her, and he was amused.

"Shall I tell you that you're very young, Cathy?" he said.

"I'm beginning to despise you."

"You're caught up in the village fever, but the world outside isn't running your kind of temperature. The trip down Blood Alley to Hong Kong isn't going to be a Sunday excursion."

"Really."

"There are the Reds on this side and trigger-happy Nationalists on the other, and down around Bias Bay we might run into a few real old-fashioned, nonpolitical cutthroats. Providing, of course, your gingerbread ferry ever gets that far."

Her tawny sweater looked almost golden in the fresh sunlight. "I promise to send you a postcard from Hong Kong."

"Why not the patrol boat instead of the ferry? You'd have speed and a few guns."

"That should be obvious, Captain Wilder. The patrol boat isn't large enough for a hundred and eighty people, plus pigs, chickens, dogs, and several trained canaries."

"You're not taking the Communist family, are you?"

"They don't know it, but yes, the Fengs are going too, Captain Wilder."

He sat back. "That should make it very interesting."

"You needn't look so superior. They'd be held responsible if we left them behind. They'd all be killed."

"Mr. Tso looks after everyone, doesn't he?"

"It's his job. Don't underestimate our *ti-pao*, Captain Wilder."

"Look—a freighter, then. Anything but that

goddamned ferryboat."

The scorn in her eyes lightened at his choice of a word; it seemed to tell her that she was winning her points, and a smile touched her lips. "The river's not deep enough to bring a freighter to Chiku Shan. We'd look rather remarkable, don't you think, trouping down to Amoy in all our numbers to go aboard?"

"You've got it all down, haven't you? Like a catechism."

She shrugged. She was absurdly sure of herself, he thought, and he admired her for it. She was sure she could taunt him into setting aside his judgment. She was sure she could remake his mind in the image of her own, and he thought that just slightly preposterous. At the same time her freshness and independence charmed him, and he couldn't feel any anger.

"How long have you lived in Chiku Shan, Cathy?"

"Seven years."

"Tell me more."

"There's not much more. Dad set up a practice along the river villages just after the war. Somehow when the Reds came along, he just couldn't leave. You're not like my father."

"I'm sure I'm a great disappointment to you."

"Dad wouldn't desert his patients. He felt responsible for them, the really sick ones, but you're different. You look after yourself."

"The truth," Wilder said easily, "will get you nowhere."

It was true that he had gone through life with a certain unhappy aloofness. It was hard for him to remember a time when he hadn't been alone. He'd been born into the clannish Shanghai world of the twenties and he'd always seemed alone in the big house off Bubbling Well Road. At school he was a head taller than the others, and because of a growing contempt, he made the worst grades. He'd finally taken a square look at the world and found it crooked. He decided not to change it. He was content to go through life as a sort of amateur spectator, grinning at its insanities and feeling nothing of its passions. It was still his way.

"When will your father get back?"

"I don't know," Cathy said. "He was taken down to Swatow to operate on some commissar or other. The Red brass knows better than to trust the People's butchers."

"You're a British subject," Wilder said. "He should have been able to get you out of China by snipping a little Red tape. Didn't he try?"

Her eyes avoided him. "Of course. My papers came through two years ago. But they wouldn't let Dad out. They need good doctors, even if they won't admit it, and they'll hold on to Dad until he works himself to death."

"You wouldn't leave without him, is that it?"

Their eyes met. "I'm sure," she said resentfully, "you consider that noble and a bit foolish."

"Cut it out." He grinned. "What does your father think about the village escape?"

"He's agreed to it."

"Does he realize you will all very possibly be killed?"

"I'm going to take Koxinga for a walk."

She whistled and Koxinga roused from under the table. She got his leash, and it seemed to Wilder there was something of the tomboy left in her movements, as if she hadn't entirely thrown off the unsophistication of her teens. Good God, he thought, she must have been in blonde pigtails when the war broke out and he was on his way up through the foc's'le. Yet, as he watched her now, she was undeniably a grown woman in a tartan skirt and loose-fitting sweater. She wore her inexperience like a chip on her shoulder, but she seemed to have a sure sense of balance.

"I'm going with you," he said.

She shrugged, and he wondered how long it had been since she had seen another Western face besides her father's.

The sun was well up above the forest and shafts of light shot down through the crenelations in the thick village wall. Cathy moved along briskly and an uneasy silence came between them. She hardly came to his shoulder, and he felt suddenly lank and awkward beside her. They worked their way up the terrace steps and Wilder could hear a singsong burst of school children already at their lessons in the temple. He made no attempt to straighten out his thoughts now. It felt too good to stretch his legs and breathe the pine-scented air. A captain's responsibility for a floating village, creeping blind along an enemy coast, didn't appeal to him. It staggered him. His cargo would be human life, not bales of rubber or drums of oil. But it was either throw in with them or abandon them, and he didn't want to think about it at all.

"Was jail so very bad?" she asked suddenly.

"The view was fine."

"I should think you'd be terribly bitter. I'm sure I would."

He let it go. He hadn't felt bitterness. There had been angers and frustrations, but he'd kept his prison behavior rigidly correct. The guards had been pompous little men and they hadn't been able to touch him with their righteous tempers and sneers and threats. Bitterness, no. But losing his ship was something else. For the first time he had known cold humiliation and he was still carrying that around inside him, and he had no intention of talking about it.

A chattering expedition of women, obviously heading for the lagoon with their baskets of wash, greeted Cathy and ignored Wilder completely. When they had passed, Cathy gave him a grin.

"You might as well get used to being snubbed. You're an invisible man as far as they're concerned."

"Mr. Tso's orders?"

"No one will have to lie to the authorities if no one has seen you."

"I suppose," Wilder said, "it figures."

"Mr. Tso's word is law—except to the Feng family. You'll have to watch out for our village Communists. Old Feng Chan-ma would report you in a minute."

"I don't intend to give him the chance." Wilder took some comfort in the power of Mr. Tso's word. The headman in a pre-Red village had unquestioned obedience, and Chiku Shan, as far as Wilder could tell, hadn't given up the old-fashioned ways. But he also knew that he was a one-man plague as far as the village was concerned; if he were discovered hiding in Chiku Shan, everyone—with the possible exception of the Fengs—would share the guilt. "What about the Fengs' servants? Are they underfoot or did they go to that funeral too?"

"The Fengs don't have any servants. They're all happy little comrades under one roof."

"I'm surprised the Reds haven't kicked Mr. Tso out and made Mr. Feng the headman."

"They tried, and then dear Mr. Feng had a dream—very realistic, you understand—that his throat was about to be cut. He quickly lost his ambition to become the *ti-pao*."

"So. Quite so."

They walked in the shadow of the rambling old wall and Wilder enjoyed the strange awareness of a woman beside him again. She wore no perfume, but there was the clean scent of soap and scrubbing about her.

"It's not bad, being an invisible man," he said after a moment. "Every third step I feel as if I'm walking through a wall. I keep wanting to turn around and start the other way. Funny."

"It seems unfair to have brought you to a walled city after all that, doesn't it?"

"At least the walls are farther apart."

When they reached the open village gates they stopped and looked down at the leaf-shaped lagoon, now a deep blue. Several women were already at the rocks of the shore, beating clothes.

"I go swimming there in the summertime," Cathy said. "You can swim at Repulse Bay, if your ferry ever gets to Hong Kong."

"I shall make a point of it," he answered brusquely. Looking down, he saw a couple of men at the landing putting boulders aboard the three fishing junks.

"I don't understand," he said finally.

She turned. "Those rocks will help us escape."

She left him standing and he watched a moment longer. He saw one of the men cover the small cargo of rocks with a fishing net and then the junk shoved off. Wilder rubbed his neck thoughtfully and a moment later caught up with Cathy and the dog.

"I don't see much sense in it."

"It's one of our secrets, Captain Wilder," she said. "And you're still an outsider."

He grinned and said to hell with it. "Look, has everyone in the village—except the Fengs, of course—been told an escape is in the works?"

"Yes."

"Isn't that risky?"

"Apparently you don't know the Chinese very well. Everyone but the children knows and everyone has things to do." She pointed toward a ragged stone watchtower farther along the wall. "Shall we go up there and sit? It's one of my favorite spots."

They went up the open stairway, the stones worn and split and tufted with weeds. A wind caught them when they reached the top, and Cathy unsnapped Koxinga's leash.

"No one comes up here but me anymore," Cathy said. The sagging rooftops of the village spread out below them and Wilder saw that here and there weeds had taken hold between the tiles. She led him into the squat, roofless tower. "I usually walk Koxinga all the way around the top. It's like a wonderful ancient highway along here, isn't it?"

The wind was in her hair and for a moment he felt as if they were standing above the world, removed and apart from it, and he was glad he had come. "You love it here in Chiku Shan, don't you, Cathy?"

She stood at one of the crenels, her legs set, her back toward him. "Sometimes." After a moment she tossed her head, turning to face him, and her eyes had changed. "But sometimes I hate it. Sometimes I feel that if I have to stay here another day I'll turn to stone, like everything else in Chiku Shan."

He sensed again that there was some secret rage inside her, but he said nothing, and she didn't go on. The moment passed, somehow unresolved, and he thought it was just as well.

Once again he noticed the old Rolls-Royce standing on its rims on the terrace below Dr. Grainger's compound. Its brightwork gleamed in the sun, and as he watched a chicken settled on one of the headlights.

"Would you have to break a blood oath," he said, pointing, "to tell me what the devil that's doing in the village?"

She leaned against the battlement and held her hair

against the wind. "That's dear Mr. Feng's gift to Chiku Shan. He sits in it a good part of the day, even when it rains sometimes, and his sons and grandsons keep it polished. He's the richest man in the village."

"He sounds crazy."

"He's far from that. He saw what was coming and joined the party even before the Reds took Shanghai. He hoped that if he were one of them, when the time came, the comrades might let him hold onto his money. He managed to, what's more. Being the family elder, he ordered all the Fengs to join up."

"And naturally they did."

"Right down to the nephews of the tenth power. There are really only four families in the village, not counting Dad and me."

"Does the car still run?"

She shook her head with a little smile. "The Japs took the engine and rubber long ago. But it was too much trouble getting the body back down the cliff, so they just left it."

"He must feel like a big wheel sitting down there, even without the engine."

"It's really not too unusual for Fukien. Dad once had a patient upriver who had a solid-gold bird cage for his trained larks. Things like that. The province was really quite poor because of all the mountains and no place much to farm, and then it got rich and things like Mr. Feng and his Rolls-Royce happened. Most of the men went away years ago on the coolie ships and they sent their families money. Everyone got horribly lazy, I guess. A lot of men came home rich to retire, and everybody was very happy that the province was so poor to start with or they might never have gone away in the first place."

"How did Mr. Feng make all his money?"

"No one knows that—or where he keeps it. He went

out as a coolie to the Philippines and when he came home his Rolls-Royce came with him. I guess that was sometime in the twenties. It's been sitting down there ever since, and so has he. I daresay there'll be quite a fine scene when it comes time for him to leave it behind." She gave Wilder a wry glance. "I'm looking forward to it."

"It sounds like you're going to have to kidnap him to get him on that ferry."

"That," she said, "is exactly what's planned for him."

"Look—I'm impressed with your Mr. Tso, but I have the feeling he has two sets of explanations for everything, like a shopkeeper with two sets of books. The Reds aren't necessarily going to assume the ferry set course for Formosa, giving you clear sailing to Hong Kong. It would make a good deal more sense to *go* to Formosa because it's a devil of a lot closer."

"Mr. Tso doesn't like long explanations, so he makes up simple ones."

"Well?"

"Chiang is on Formosa. Chiku Shan wasn't much better off under the Nationalists than it is under the Reds. Mr. Tso and Company don't want any more of either. The answer is Hong Kong."

"There must be a better reason for the ferry."

"There is. One of Mr. Tso's nephews is the chief engineer."

Chapter Four

He decided not to stretch out on the bed. Fatigue had settled in his bones and he wasn't sure he could stay awake unless he stayed on his feet. He spread the shutters wide and peered at the silted river, almost cinnamon in the sparkling morning sunlight. The amah, Susu, had taken away the uniform and brought him a pot of scented Anhui tea, and he could hear her busy at work below. He had left Cathy along the battlements. He couldn't put off his decision much longer, and he knew he had to get away from her for that.

What, after all, did he remember of the coast? In the years since the Reds took over he had been on the southern run to Singapore, and now the coast north of Hong Kong became a long, rocky blur in his mind.

He turned from the window, and the plank flooring squeaked under his feet. Cathy had seen through him very quickly, if not too clearly, he thought, and now her remarks left him mildly disturbed. They were obsessed, all of them, with a doomed escape plan, and she took his hesitation for selfishness and his caution as the way of a coward.

But he supposed they were no madder than the rest of China. He remembered his father and the other Shanghai taipans, arrogant, preening men with their minds on the cash register and an ingenious appetite for luxury. He could not recall ever having seen his father, a descendant of a hard-drinking China captain of the opium-trade years, put on his own shoes before going off to his shipping office on the Bund. That was the duty of the number-three boy, and Wilder had always found these little morning scenes both painful and preposterous. Later, when he had been expelled from every school in Shanghai and sent off to the States to try college, the Japs had come, and finally his father had died in a concentration camp. Even now, Wilder remembered the barbed-wire picture that often sprang into his head—all those Shanghai taipans struggling to put on their own shoes.

Except for his ship and his crew, Wilder had come to feel no responsibility for the world he lived in. He didn't care to distinguish himself. He was indifferent to the opinions of others. He'd found a way of life that suited him.

But he didn't like to be thought a coward.

He shrugged and, turning back to the windows, saw Cathy and the terrier walking around the top of the village wall. Dr. Grainger must be something of a fool, he thought. He had risked Cathy's life and his own to stay behind and tend a handful of patients out of almost five hundred million Chinese. Wilder had met these men trying to be Davids to China's Goliath, and they were always bores.

But Wilder turned away from his thoughts with a sense of guilt. At least Dr. Grainger had demonstrated a certain courage, and Wilder knew that he himself had never quite put his own courage, or even his abilities, to the test. It had never seemed worthwhile.

After a moment he stopped walking the floor, aware suddenly that the amah below could hear the wooden squeaks as he paced. He straddled a small chair and finally he began to grin. There was no denying it, the Reds would lose face if one of their ancient villages transplanted itself from the banks of the Dragon River to the banks of free Hong Kong. It would humiliate the commissars; it would settle an old score. His caution of the last hour abruptly deserted him.

He stood up from the chair and opened the bedroom door.

"Susu!" he yelled.

The amah appeared a moment later at the bottom of the stairs.

"Don't come up," Wilder snapped. "Get me the largest sheet of paper you can find and something to write with. A big piece of paper, you understand? Big as a window!"

"My catchee!" She went off, her hands flying.

During the next few moments Wilder felt a grim sort of—exhilaration. He dredged his memory for the thousands of submerged rocks, the passages and reefs that lay between Amoy and Hong Kong. He remembered the pass between Flying Fish and Ching Rocks, just south of Amoy, and the shoal off Cone Point. The Swatow landmarks began popping into his head—Halftide Reef and Three Chimney Bluff and Breaker Point.

The amah brought him a mechanical pencil with "Wing On Life Assurance Co., Ltd." stamped on its side, and a sheet of paper the size of a windowpane. Wilder shook his head and went downstairs himself.

He found a brass inkwell and writing brush in Dr. Grainger's study, and, despite Susu's alarms, carried off a large medical chart depicting the nervous system of the human body.

Back in his own room, he locked the door and set to work. He turned over the chart, spreading the blank side across the bed, and lettered "Amoy" at the upper right-hand corner. Then he tried to imagine the gently convex coastline to the lower left-hand corner and "Hong Kong." He remembered now the twin peninsulas ending in Black Head and Thunder Head, and, backtracking, he put in an ink mark for Chapel Island as he recalled the black tower and white stone wall of the lighthouse. He reached Swatow and had to stop. Outside of the few points that had come to mind at once, the area was a rambling confusion of islands, rocks, and bays. It offered dozens of hiding places, and they ought to reach it by the end of the second night. After inking in the spread of river mouths, he skipped to the first of the four large bays that scalloped the coast above Hong Kong. He lost track of time as memories flooded in on him. He remembered coming into Mirs Bay one night and ramming the fishing stakes that made a pincushion of the place. Where was Pedro Blanco—outside of Bias Bay or Honghai Bay? He put in the lighthouse at Chilang Point and saw again the jagged rock and red sand of the shoreline. But still, there were miles that remained lost in his head. He worked up and down the rough coast, adding details as they came to him. Thumb Rock. Goat Island. Hogsback Islet. The Ninepin Group. He remembered the sound of the fog gun from Breaker Point Lighthouse; somewhere near there, he thought, he'd have to watch out for a couple of dangerous wrecks.

When finally Wilder straightened, he had no idea what time it was. Mr. Tso must be getting impatient. Wilder's eyes burned and his muscles ached; he had to get some sleep. But he was pleased with the rough chart on the bed, even though there were too many blank stretches to leave him entirely satisfied. He stared at the thing, amazed that he'd been able to remember that much. Well, there had to be more. He'd keep working on it.

He felt the teapot. Cold. He'd have a cup of hot tea and hit the sack. He glanced at the chart again. Maybe they had a chance, even on that turtle of a ferryboat. He rolled up the chart and stood it in a corner of the room. He unlocked the door.

"Susu!"

It wasn't the amah that answered. Cathy appeared at the foot of the stairway, glancing up at him with a very crisp smile. "You wanchee velly numba-one wash amah?"

"Never mind Susu." He grinned. "Tell Mr. Tso him catchee velly numba-one boat captain."

"That won't be necessary," she said, tossing back her hair. "I already have."

Chapter Five

He was awakened by a pounding at the door.

He sat up quickly and the room was entirely strange: the plaster walls, the open windows, the sun striking the bedstead, polished brass, and the clean smell.

"Tom—you must wake up!"

A woman's voice. He remembered now. Cathy's voice. Dr. Grainger's house. Chiku Shan. He couldn't have been asleep more than an hour, and he felt worse than before.

"Tom—"

"I'm awake."

"You must get out of here! Hurry!"

"What?"

She beat on the door again, and there was a catch of alarm in her voice. "They've just come round into the lagoon—a boatload of soldiers. Please hurry! They'll be starting a search in minutes."

Wilder tossed aside his blanket and pulled on his trousers. He got into the straw sandals and remembered the gun. He felt for it under the pillow and shoved it into his pocket. He opened the door.

"They couldn't have traced me," he said.

"They must have." She looked different. She still wore the tartan skirt and the loose, tawny sweater, but the casual air was gone. Her glance was quick and earnest. She took his hand and pulled him down the stairs with her. "Mr. Tso's waiting for you. This house is one of the first they're apt to search."

Mr. Tso greeted him with the hasty suggestion of a bow and forced a smile on his broad, deep-cut face. "We regret—"

"I understand."

"The temple will be safest for you. We have planned it so. Follow me quickly, please."

Wilder squinted in the sudden brightness of the courtyard. They rushed along the stone walks and Mr. Tso's gray silk gown flew. They passed no one; nothing in the village seemed to move but blue cotton laundry in the breeze.

"This way, this way."

The temple, squat and austere, faced south, like all the buildings in the village. It stood on the highest level, behind its own walls, and as they approached Wilder saw that mango birds had built their nests under the swooping corners of the temple roof.

"It was not expected they would search our village so soon," Mr. Tso said in a worried tone. "Still, it matters little. The hawks and dogs will leave with their mouths empty."

Wilder said nothing. His own safety meant very little, he knew. It was Chiku Shan that was at stake.

He followed the elder through a moon gate in the outer temple wall. They strode across an open courtyard and the incense of joss sticks hung over the place like a mist.

"Is it unthinkable that one of your villagers may have informed the authorities?" Wilder muttered.

Mr. Tso's glance was sharp and piercing. "It is unthinkable," he replied flatly.

School was still in session in one of the rooms of the temple, and the strident voices of children, shouting their lessons in unison, rang out over the village. Mr. Tso unlocked a great door at the back of the temple and led Wilder into a hall-like room with ancient teak beams and a single high window. Once Wilder saw the rows of coffins, lacquered and extravagantly carved, he saw little else. The smell of burned candles and incense was sweet and overpowering.

Many of the coffins, Wilder knew at once, were not empty. Even the village dead had to wait on the calculations of the devil doctor. Until the *suan-ming-ti* reckoned the harmonious time and place for burial, according to the rigid principles of wind and water, they'd have to wait it out in the temple storeroom. The empty woodwork, Wilder knew, was merely so much personal property. Coffins bought early, or received as gifts, waiting for their owners.

"I'm to stay here?" Wilder said blandly.

"You will be safe among our honored ancestors."

Mr. Tso removed the heavy, overhanging lid of a bright red coffin and pointed out concealed air holes from the inside. "This has been prepared for such emergencies, yes?"

"I'll be all right."

"You will be safe, yes."

The coffin was lined in cedar and Wilder was thankful for its freshening scent. He stretched out on silk pillows and Mr. Tso pulled the lid over him. A moment later he could hear the elder's receding footsteps, and then he was alone.

He remained indifferent to the macabre interior of a coffin; his attitude toward the dead was entirely Oriental. He thought, instead, of the voyage, and names started repeating themselves through his mind. Goat Island. Thunder Head. Pedro Blanco. Where the hell was Pedro Blanc—

He froze.

The chart. The last he'd seen of it, the damned thing was standing in the corner of the bedroom.

He'd left it there!

For a moment he only lay there thinking it through. In their nosy way, the search party would find it. They couldn't really miss it. An X mark for Amoy and an X mark for Hong Kong and even a buffoon in bandoliers could figure out that an escape was on someone's mind. Who in Chiku Shan but that running dog of a sea captain would have filled in all those lighthouses and shoals and rocks?

Wilder shoved up on the coffin lid and forced it aside. He had to get to the bedroom before the comrades did. It was going to take them a little time to get their search organized, and all he needed was a little time.

He felt the stone floor under his feet again and cursed himself for leaving the chart behind. He hurried past the silent coffins and reached the big door.

But Mr. Tso had locked it behind him.

Chapter Six

The high window was barred.

Wilder froze, but his mind raced. Cathy *must* have gone over his room. It would be disastrous if she'd rushed past her father's medical chart, standing in the corner. He couldn't take the risk. He began to work, quickly. He wrapped a silk coffin pillow snugly around the gun in his hand and shot the brass door lock. The door parted on its dry hinges and the muffled explosion growled through the room like a deep-throated firecracker.

He felt the sun on his shoulders.

He avoided the bright expanse of the temple courtyard, climbing the rubble in a V-shaped chink in the crumbling old wall. Below and off to his left he would see the glazed green roof of Dr. Grainger's house.

A chicken flew out of his path and flowerpots lined his way. There was a distant jabbering in the air; soldiers, he knew, fanning out from the village gate on the north side of Chiku Shan.

He flattened himself against a damp courtyard wall,

checked the intersecting stone lane, and then all but skidded to the lower terrace. He reached Dr. Grainger's walls, assured himself the compound was deserted, and ran to the house.

The door was locked.

He rapped quickly.

The house stood rigidly still. He knocked again. After an impatient moment he abandoned the door. Where the hell was everyone? He worked his way around to the back of the house, trying windows, and found one unlocked. He hoisted himself into the house and closed the shutters after him.

"Cathy!"

His voice echoed through an empty house. He didn't take time to try to figure it out. He hurried up the wooden stairs and got into his room.

The chart was missing from the corner.

He let out a breath. The bed had been made up. He stood for a moment in the center of the room and knew he'd been a fool. He grinned wryly. Did he think he'd been issued the only set of uncracked brains in the village of Chiku Shan? Cathy had hidden the chart and straightened up every trace of him.

Why hadn't he trusted her to do that?

He moved again. He'd walked himself out on a crazy limb and he wondered if there was time to walk himself back. He got to the windows and peered down through the shutter. He saw patches of mustard green on the move through the lanes. The place was lousy with uniforms now. Fine. He must have had his brains washed without knowing it.

He whirled at the sound of movement under his feet.

Someone below. Footsteps in the house, on the loose-jointed stairway. A hushed voice.

"Captain Wilder."

He crossed to the open doorway.

Cathy stopped midway up the stairway when she saw him. She had been taking the stairs two at a time, her skirt pulled above her knees, and she looked entirely young and untamed. She dropped her skirt and swung back her hair. "I saw you come over here."

"It was slightly less than brilliant."

"Are you trying to ruin everything?"

"Let's say I was a damned fool and let it go at that."

"You mustn't stay in this house."

"I think I'd better."

"But—"

"There's got to be somewhere."

She hesitated a moment and finished climbing the stairs. "My room," she said decisively.

"All right," he said. "Your room."

She moved past him, her hair loose and straw-colored in the gloom of the shuttered house. Her eyes avoided him and he sensed her impatience and resentment. She must despise him for coming back, he thought, but maybe she liked these opportunities to display her range of emotions. He shrugged wearily and followed her along the hall.

"Mr. Tso told us to lock up the house and to stay with the Han family," she said. "That's when we saw you pass."

"Mr. Tso thinks of everything."

"He didn't want Susu and me to be alone in the house when the comrades searched us. They're not always"—she turned the knob of her door—"well mannered."

"Where is he?"

"At the gate, welcoming the heroes."

"You'd better get back to the Hans'. I'll be all right."

"I'll stay."

He caught her wrist to stop her. "Look, don't be a

fool just because I was. Go back to the Hans'. I can take care of myself. Get going."

Her eyes blazed and she slapped him.

"Don't *ever* try ordering me around, Captain Wilder. And take your hands off me."

He rubbed his cheek and tried not to grin. She must have been hoping for an excuse to let fly, and she hadn't had to wait long. "I have unhanded you," he said easily. "You stay."

"Thank you."

Her bedroom was almost as austere as his own. There was the same uncovered plank floor, the plaster walls and the shutters in need of paint. He did see a dressing table with a slick black flounce of "fragrant-cloud linen," but there were no perfume bottles, no cosmetics—merely a comb sitting in a brush. The bed, however, looked like plunder out of a museum. It was a tasseled four-poster affair with a faded silk canopy and embroidered dragons. It seemed remarkably out of place and oversized for the room.

"Maybe you'll fit under my dressing table," Cathy said, after a quick survey of possibilities. "If they come looking in here, I'll manage to keep them away somehow."

"That's quite a piece of real estate you sleep in."

She turned, facing him sharply. "Do you realize this is quite serious?"

"Sorry."

"I'm sure you had a marvelous reason for coming back."

He picked up a small doll propped against the dressing table mirror. "It seemed important at the time." The doll, no longer than his hand and brightly dyed, was impaled on a stick. He twirled it. The legs and arms whirled and the figure danced. Something clicked in his mind. He remembered a windy day just after the war when he'd stood watching a Chinese making these things on the steps of the Sea View Hotel in Amoy. He'd put them together out of rice flour, baking them over charcoal, and Wilder had been impressed with the man's frivolous artistry. Now it depressed him a little, as he twirled the stick and watched the bright-eyed little figure perform. It seemed somehow a part of the old China that would never come back.

"I got rattled, I guess. I was afraid you might not notice the chart I'd left behind. Where did you get this?"

"One of our families makes them. The Sings. I had Susu take your chart to the kitchen and burn it in the oven."

The doll froze in his fingers. "What?"

"If they'd found your—"

"You didn't have to burn it." He tossed the doll back against the mirror.

"There wasn't time to find an absolutely safe place. It seemed better simply to destroy it."

He turned away. He could make another. He might have admired her directness, but he felt there was something vindictive in what she had done and it made him angry. There was a clatter below in the courtyard and Cathy hurried to the shutters.

"We're getting company."

She left him standing.

A moment later he could hear voices drifting up from the lower floor of the house. Wilder remained in the open bedroom doorway and listened to Mr. Tso's politely protesting voice.

"We hide no one, *ta-jên*. As one can see, this—"

"*Hsiu-shuo!*"

"There is an unfortunate error," Mr. Tso persisted easily. "Your information—"

"*Hsiu-shuo*, old wine sack! We know you lie."

The search went tumbling like an ill wind through the lower part of the house. There must be half a dozen of them, Wilder thought. He left the doorway, picked up the dancer on the stick, and folded himself under the dressing table. He adjusted the black flounce to conceal him, rested the gun in the crease of his lap, and twirled the stick. The doll whirled like a dervish. He found it remarkable and amusing that one of the Chiku Shan families were dollmakers. Well, they could make their Amoy dolls in Hong Kong.

He passed the time watching the rice-flour arms and legs swing and was glad for something to busy his fingers. Finally voices came into the room with him and he stopped.

"This is where I sleep," Cathy said crisply. "Do look under the bed. I believe that's the classic hiding place."

"You joke, girl?" Nasal.

"In the People's Republic, one never jokes."

There were two soldiers with her. Wilder could hear them padding around as Cathy sat at the dressing table. Her sandals almost touched his ribs and apparently she began brushing her hair.

"But you are wrong, girl." Nasal and sweetening. "In the People's Republic finally we have much to joke about. You English are very funny, eh?"

The voice was near. Wilder thought the soldier talking must be standing at Cathy's back.

"Take your hands off me," she said coolly.

"But I am only joking. Have you English no sense of humor, eh?"

"You came to search this room—not me."

"Am I not handsome, girl? Have you seen one as handsome as Wang? Come, look."

Wilder could smell the acrid sweat from the soldier's tennis shoes only inches away.

"You're pulling my hair," Cathy said quietly.

"Look at me, girl!"

"Get out or I shall scream for your officer downstairs."

"You prefer him to me?"

The other soldier broke in with a laugh. "Where did you learn to make love, Wang—in a drill book? Come, there are other rooms to search."

"She is modest with a long-eared bumpkin like you watching," Wang said with a faint sneer. "A girl likes to be alone at such a time, even in a willow house. *Ai*, it is unfortunate we have other things to do. Come, girl! Perhaps I will make you smile yet."

A few moments later their voices were down the hall and sweat was dripping off the end of Wilder's nose. For the first time he could understand the impulse to murder.

"They traced you to the village," Cathy said nervously.

Mr. Tso and the comrades had moved on. The house was still, but Wilder could feel Wang's presence in the bedroom yet, and the smell of his tennis shoes.

"I'm sorry," Wilder said. "I'm sorry I didn't kill him."

"Don't be a fool. He was only trying to show off. It wasn't important. Look, they saw you—I mean the sampan—from the ferryboat last night. They say the ferry almost ran down a sampan about the time you escaped from Kulangsu, and they reason that must be how you got off the island. They've traced the sampan to Chiku Shan."

"It's a long shot."

"Of course they're not absolutely sure, even if they act that way. But one of the sailors remembered the smell of the sampan—fertilizer—when the ferry skimmed past. They've checked the fertilizer companies in Amoy and now they're following up the few sampans that bought loads yesterday."

"What else?"

"Well, they're really turning the village upside down. And they're trying to thrash answers out of Little Han."

"Little Han?"

"The coolie who brought you."

Wilder's eyes tightened. "I'm sorry."

"He's been beaten before. He won't talk."

"It's not something you get used to."

"He volunteered to pick you up at Kulangsu and he knew the risks he was taking. No, he won't give you away."

Wilder rubbed the back of his neck. The treatment Little Han had earned on his account filled Wilder with an icy frustration. It had been the same thing sitting behind the fragrant-cloud linen while Cathy got pawed by a green pig in tennis shoes.

"I'll be glad to get out of here," he said sharply. Until the stern-wheeler was taken, he was only in the way.

She smiled soothingly. "Tomorrow we'll have the ferry. It'll be easier for you then."

"Has it occurred to anyone that I'll need a crew?"

"I'm sure Mr. Tso is providing for it."

"Will your father be back in time?"

The words slipped off his tongue and left him feeling like an idiot. In that moment he saw what he hadn't seen before: She was worried. She turned away and tried to pass it off with a smile. "Dad's never late for trains or boats. Maybe he'll get back tonight. It's been two weeks, but I never know when to expect him. I'm not worried. Dad has a way of turning up."

"Cathy—" He stopped short.

She turned back to him and their gazes froze.

"There's someone downstairs," he muttered quickly.

There was a brittle trail of noises as if a drunk had got loose in the furniture.

And then Wang's oily voice shot through the house. "Girl!"

All right, Wilder thought, Wang had detached himself from the others and come back. They didn't need the village prophet to figure out why.

"Girl! You are upstairs, eh?"

Cathy started across the bedroom toward the door; Wilder caught her shoulders in his fingers and stopped her. Their eyes clashed savagely, and then she wrenched away. She left him standing and disappeared along the hall. His palms began to sweat.

He could hear the heavy squeaking of the stairway; Wang was coming up. And then Cathy's voice, sure and self-possessed, came like a crack of distant thunder.

"Get out."

"But I have just come, girl."

"Then I shall just leave."

Wang laughed. "We are alone now, eh? Come, girl, you don't fool me. Ten thousand women in Amoy dream of ten minutes alone with Wang."

"Perhaps it is only Wang dreaming of ten thousand women. This is not a willow-lane house, *t'ung-chih*. Get out."

Wilder stood where he was. She was a cool article and maybe she'd pull it off.

Mockery came into Wang's voice. "Is it not your duty, girl, to serve the People's heroes?"

"Let me pass."

Wang's laughter turned savage. "Eggs do not quarrel with stones."

"You're blocking my way."

A purr. "We are alone, eh?"

Wilder managed to keep his hand off the Tokarev.

Another shot in the village wouldn't pass unnoticed, not this time.

"Your comrade heroes will miss you," Cathy said sharply. "Don't make a fool of yourself for my benefit."

There was no panic in her voice. Wilder could have tossed him out by the scruff of the neck, but he knew that once he exposed himself to Wang, he'd have to kill him.

"There are so many, this hero won't be missed for ten minutes."

"Do you always carry a rifle when you call on a woman?"

"*K'uai-lai!* You should be honored that I call on one, such as you, with so little flesh." He burst into an impatient laugh. "But a good soldier is impartial."

Cathy's temper exploded and proverbs ran off her tongue in the Chinese way. "Vile earth duck! Get out of my house! When is good iron made into nails or good men into soldiers?"

"You will see what a good soldier is Wang! *Ju-shish! Ju-shih!*"

There was the sound of scuffling in the hall together with Cathy's suddenly muffled voice. Wilder's temples throbbed. What if it were only a trick, with other soldiers below in the house, waiting for the American to crawl out of the woodwork? Had they come to suspect, somehow, that he was in the house?

But when Cathy's sob broke free of Wang's hand, Wilder ignored his sense of caution.

He went through the doorway and gazed along the hall.

Wang's fuzzy green back was toward him; he was trying to pin Cathy to the plank floor with one dirty tennis shoe hard across her mouth.

"*Hsiu-shuo!*"

The bayonet flashed in the wooden gloom. Wang, his

breath loud in the hall, worked quickly with the rifle, ripping open Cathy's tartan skirt, and shouted again. "*Hsiu-shuo*, girl!"

He jammed the point of the bayonet into the floor with a dull thud, and the rifle stood at an angle. He grabbed Cathy's golden hair in his fist, removing his foot from across her face. He bent over her, looking in his green uniform like the earth duck Cathy had called him—a frog.

Wilder's blood coursed. Wang, deafened by his own purring laughter, was unaware until the moment Wilder reached him.

The last thing the Chinese saw was the dull gleam of his bayonet.

Wilder gutted him.

Chapter Seven

Wilder supposed it was the worst fifteen minutes of his life. Cathy stood against the wall, sobbing through the trap of her fingers, her eyes gazing at him with vacant horror.

"Better get out of here," he said.

"I can—"

He picked her bright skirt off the floor and threw it at her. "Just get the hell out."

The shadow of hysteria passed from her green eyes, but she didn't move. There was no time to lose. Wang might have boasted to his comrades of what he was up to, and someone might come looking for him. Every second counted now. Wang had to be got out of sight.

"Let me—"

"I'll do it alone," Wilder snapped.

Cathy, her face terribly white, moved on her sandaled feet, and a moment later Wilder heard her bedroom door softly close. He stared down at the short, stocky figure at his feet. A pack of cigarettes had pitched out of the soldier's pocket and lay now like an island in a swelling pool of blood. They were Chien Mens, Wilder saw, the cheap brand Mao himself had smoked since his days in the loess caves of Shensi province. He supposed every crumby comrade with ambitious military fancies had switched to Chien Mens.

Wilder made a quick search of the house and returned upstairs with a laundry basket. Five minutes later Wang was hidden in the kitchen under a pile of wet clothes. Then Wilder cleaned up the hall, wiped off the bayonet, and hid the rifle under the mattress of his bed.

Then he waited.

But no one came.

An hour later the soldiers cleared out. The village heaved a sigh of relief and returned chuckling to the day's work. When the amah returned, Wilder warned her away from the laundry basket and sent her to bring Mr. Tso. Alone again in the disheveled living room, he knew he had placed the entire escape in jeopardy. Wang had apparently kept his amorous thoughts to himself before sneaking off to the Grainger house, but he would be missed somewhere along the line. And there was sure to be a follow-up.

Wilder busied himself straightening up the furniture and kept glancing at the stairway. Cathy hadn't come out of her room and he supposed she wouldn't until the redness had gone out of her eyes. None of this would have happened, he reflected uneasily, if he had stuck to the temple in the first place. Cathy would have been safe with the Han ménage and Wang would be on the little scow heading back for Amoy.

When Susu got back she was alone. Mr. Tso had

called together the elders for a meeting. He'd be along later.

Wilder went upstairs and knocked at Cathy's door. There was no answer, and finally he turned the knob.

She was standing at the shuttered window, her slim back framed between the tall bedposts, and he saw that she had changed into a blouse and lavender corduroy slacks. A wide golden belt gave a trim look to the narrow structure of her hips and her willowy legs.

"They're gone," Wilder said.

"I know."

"Cathy—"

"I'm all right," she said coolly.

He crossed the room slowly, not certain what had been going through her mind. There was no point in brooding over what might have been. She had watched a man skewered like a pig and it had made a shocking sight. All right, he thought, it hadn't been a pretty death, but it had been silent.

He reached past her shoulders and opened the shutters, and sunlight spread over her. Her eyes were bright blue again, her hair as golden as the belt; from the temple the voices of schoolchildren once again rose over Chiku Shan as if nothing had happened. The glazed flowerpots along the compound wall below sparkled.

"Let's forget it," Wilder said. "Look—stuff the typhoon ripped up is still floating down the river."

But she didn't look at the river; she looked up at him and her voice was firm. "I'm not very good at saying thank you."

"Then don't bother."

"I suppose you were very heroic."

"Cut it out," he said.

"You were very cool and efficient."

"I'm not very proud of myself, if that's what's bothering you. I'm sorry if I was cool and efficient, if that makes me inhuman."

"Are you in love with me, Captain Wilder?"

"No," he said. "I'm not in love with you."

"Then why did you kill him?"

"It seemed like a swell idea."

"Do you suppose I'm the first woman ever touched by a soldier?"

"It didn't occur to me to wonder about it. Are you making sense?"

"I would have lived through the affair in the hall without you." She tossed back her hair and left the window. "He'll be missed at his barracks and they'll come looking for him." She turned and faced Wilder emotionally. "Don't you realize you may have ruined everything?"

"Stop kidding me, baby. You're goddamned glad I came along. As for Wang, if we have a little luck he'll be put down as AWOL for a couple of days. If we get the ferry tomorrow night, we'll be gone before they can trace him here."

Why was she trying to turn her emotions inside out? He had seen her quick moods and he thought now she was trying to hate him. Did that mean she had been crazy enough to fall in love with him? The killing had been brutal and in a way unnecessary. He might have stood by during Wang's little entertainment, but she could never get him to believe she would have preferred it. Now there was blood on his hands.

"Look, Cathy—"

"I suppose I'm making a fool of myself. Maybe you'd better go."

"I'm not through making a fool of myself. You haven't fallen in love with me, have you, Cathy?"

Her eyes flashed up and some of the brittle pretense

fell away. "You'd hate that, wouldn't you?"

"I'm damned near old enough to be your grandfather, you know."

"You're only thirty-one."

That wasn't quite what he meant and he wasn't sure he could explain it. He was impatient with naive young things; his entanglements had always been conscienceless affairs with experienced women and he'd always been able pick up his hat and leave. "We live in different worlds, Cathy. Don't let's get them mixed up. You're a nice kid and I don't want you to get hurt."

"I'm touched." She smiled grimly. "Do go on."

He knew that was his cue to leave, but he felt that he'd better say it all. "You don't know anything about me. Maybe I'd better tell you. I've never been accused of being a nice guy. You saw me kill Wang, cool and efficient, and I think it frightened you. I'll scare you some more. Once I washed up the blood, it was no strain. I cured myself of a conscience years ago. Wang is just a basket of wash to be got out of the way now. I'm really not much different than Wang, only luckier. The only reason I hated to see the Reds take China was personal—they closed a lot of ports where I had girlfriends. Chinese, Eurasians, White Russians. Sex is an international language and I've always been international as hell. I want you to understand. I'll end up on the beach with a bottle of cheap rice wine in one hand and my cap pulled down over my eyes, and maybe that's the way I want it. If we ever get to Hong Kong you'll be able to step into your own world, where you belong, and I'll get back to mine. Not that I've been missed. That's the way it's going to be, Cathy."

"Thunder roars loudly, but little rain falls."

"Go to hell."

"Tom—"

He stopped. There was a smile on her lips and he wondered if he had protested too much. He wasn't sure how much of what he had said was even the truth. All he knew for sure was that he didn't want to be bothered having her fall in love with him and he felt a need to head it off before it got started. She was young and easily impressed, hemmed in by Chinese faces, and he had walked in this morning, a lanky stranger with straight eyes and a Western tongue. She deserved more than a disenchanted thirty-one-year-old bastard, a symbol of the past, a China skipper.

"*Hsien-ch'a-mên*," Wilder said in crisp Mandarin. "When idle, drink tea. Let's drink tea."

"I think you must be a horrible liar." Cathy smiled gently from the window. "I shall try very hard to fall in love with you, because it frightens you. It's silly, of course, because I couldn't love a man without a conscience."

"Maybe this is your lucky day."

"Look, you didn't mean what you said—not caring about the Reds, I mean. You *must* care."

"Let me cat the anchor once and for all. Someone pinned the bleeding heart of China on your sleeve, but they never got around to me. We're foreigners, both of us, and what happens in China is their business. I meant it and I'm sorry if it disturbs you, baby. Look, I remember when I was a kid I used to look at the moon and try to see an old man chopping down a tree, the way the Chinese do when they look at the moon. I couldn't see it and finally I got wise. I wasn't a Chinese."

"I've always seen it."

"All right."

"Shall I tell you what I remember? I was about ten, I think. I was coming home from school and passed a ricksha coolie wailing near the Legation Quarter with one foot in his hand. He'd cut a deep gash in his arch on a piece of glass in the road. I stopped to gape at him. His eyes were horrible. You could read his thoughts in them. He knew he'd starve to death before the cut healed and he could make rice money pulling his ricksha again. He knew with a terrible certainty that he was going to die. People passed him by with only a glance. He was old and brown and ragged and others were starving in the city every day. I had some money saved for a frilly dress and ran home to fetch it. I was violently in love with a boy at school and I was sure he'd finally notice me in that dress. With the money in my hands I imagined myself pirouetting before him in my new dress. I never went back on the street with the money. I couldn't. I had to have that dress. I was a foreigner and the old coolie was none of my affair. I'm sure the death carts found him one morning in some doorway and pitched him into the wagon. And when I bought the frilly dress I couldn't bear it against my skin. I never wore it. I burned it."

"And you've been searching for that ricksha coolie ever since."

"I've found him."

Sure, he thought. One hundred and eighty ricksha coolies: the Chiku Shan village escape. Her hidden rage was an old guilt and the coming risks and dangers would purge it.

"Sure," he said.

Mr. Tso arrived as they finished lunch. His great flat face with its owlish wrinkles bore none of the genial warmth of the morning, and Wilder sensed at once that something was wrong. The meeting of the elders had taken a big chunk out of the day and Wang still lay in the wash basket.

"Forgive my lateness. There was much to discuss."

"I regret this trouble I have brought to the village," Wilder said. "Now I have added to the trouble. I have killed a soldier in this house."

The wrinkles set like tail feathers around the old man's eyes. He asked only the necessary questions. "So. Such things are sometimes necessary."

"I'm hoping," Wilder said, "that we'll be on our way before he is traced back here."

"I regret that will not be possible," Mr. Tso muttered. "We have learned from the soldiers that last night the storm claimed an unfortunate victim. Our steamboat took damage in the South River. It no longer runs."

Chapter Eight

The wash basket was moved to the temple to wait for the night. Wilder stretched out on the brass bed and tried to dismiss Wang from his mind. He tried to sleep through the afternoon, but with the Amoy ferryboat out of commission his thoughts kept him awake. How badly was it damaged? When Mr. Tso's engineering nephew returned home they would know whether they had to delay their ferryboat escape or abandon it.

It seemed strange to Wilder that he felt cheated. He had considered the little stern-wheeler absurd, but now he disliked to think of any other ship. It would be no great feat to reach Hong Kong in the armed patrol boat; his problem would be almost entirely navigational. But the paddle-wheeler, slow and vulnerable, seemed now the finest instrument of contempt and humiliation. Red China would look ridiculous when they came crashing through the bamboo curtain on a goddamned little ferryboat into

Hong Kong harbor.

He damned the typhoon and got little sleep. Mr. Tso had decided Wilder must have shoes that fitted and clothes made for his long arms and legs, and villagers broke into his afternoon to take various measurements. He'd finally given up trying to sleep at all, and with another of Dr. Grainger's medical charts had started a new map of the coast.

That night four river sampans came to Chiku Shan and word spread quickly through the village that the Feng family, thirty-eight strong, was back early from the funeral in Changchow. Wilder no longer had the freedom of the village. With the Communist Fengs once more at home, he must remain inside the Grainger house and completely out of sight.

Wilder awoke late the next morning. He opened the scaly brown shutters to let in the sun, but when the amah brought him a rice congee and tea, she pulled them shut again.

"How fashion captain sailor-man open shutter? Wanchee bad tlouble? *Yih!* Feng see captain sailor-man, you know what happen. No walkee window!"

"Maskee, maskee," Wilder muttered. She was right, of course. For the time being he'd better stay behind closed shutters and away from open windows.

Susu, buttoned to her fleshy neck in blue, cast her sharp eyes at his long hair. "My tinky captain sailor-man need cuttee heh. My cuttee ollo time doctor heh. My cuttee. Oll ligh?"

"All right," Wilder said. "Captain sailor-man also wanchee bath."

"Can do."

She left him to eat his breakfast and he stood drinking his tea at the shutters, glancing through the slats at the sun-patched village below. And he saw old

Feng, the Red elder, as thick and fat as a pumpkin, waddling across his own stone courtyard toward the Rolls-Royce on the terrace immediately below. It could be no one but Feng, he thought, a straw-hat riding on a puff of orange silk. A couple of younger Chinese walked with him, obsequiously installed him in the car, and set to work polishing the hood and fenders. The scene unfolded in utter comic silence, and Wilder had the feeling he was watching some crazy marionette show in the sun.

Cathy knocked lightly at the open door of his bedroom.

"Any news?" Wilder asked.

"None. I think you'd better come downstairs." She looked faintly worn and dispirited. "Mr. Tso has brought our *Fêng-Shui* man to see you."

"What does your crystal gazer want with me?"

"There's trouble over Wang."

"Wasn't he moved out of the village last night?"

"No. Dr. Sing made some calculations and said it was an ill-fated night to move the body."

Wilder set down his teacup.

Cathy stopped him in the hall and looked up earnestly. "Look, don't be brash with them. Their old ways are almost all they have left."

"The Reds will gut the village if they happen to find Wang's corpse here. Does Mr. Tso really go for this *Fêng-Shui* fakery?"

"I don't know. But the others do, and he honors their beliefs. I'm quite serious. Don't cross their fortuneteller." Her face was pale and he realized that the news about the ferry must have crushed her; he wondered if she'd got any sleep at all.

"Look, Cathy," he said firmly. "We're going to break out of Red China if we have to do it by sampan. But we're not going to make it by consulting an almond-eyed *suan-ming-ti* every time there's a decision to be made. Hell, these village Chinese won't grow a mustache until their fortuneteller O.K.'s it with the stars."

"Please, Tom," she said gently. "We're foreigners in China. You reminded me of that last night."

It had always amused Wilder to see the side-street astrologers with their claptrap of oracle bones and magic sands and their paper-backed Bible—the book of ten thousand years—but he wasn't amused now. "Wang needs dumping downriver and soon. It *might* keep an investigation off our backs."

"Dr. Sing says the first good day to move him is a week from tomorrow."

"That's a week too long to wait."

"Please. Mr. Tso persuaded Dr. Sing to come to you, so that you might cast a new horoscope and get a closer date if possible. They're waiting. All you have to do is—be lucky."

Mr. Tso stood impatiently flicking the comb through his starched white wisp of a beard when they appeared. He smiled quickly and the comb bounced on its ribbon. The man beside him was hardly more than half Mr. Tso's height, with coarse pomaded black hair and the sunken cheeks of an opium addict.

The introductions were flowery and the name was Dr. Sing, of the dollmaking Sing family.

The doctor of magic wore a black cotton gown and a frayed brocaded vest. He carried a chamois bag and a thin yellow book. His eyes, behind ornamental brass-rimmed glasses, were sharp and humorless. He seemed a preposterous little man. Wilder assumed the spectacles were mere glass, worn as the Oriental symbol of the intellectual. His manners were classical. As Cathy returned to the room he removed the glasses as one tips his hat. His skin was darker and he was shorter than most Chinese, as the Fukienese often are.

Tea was set before them. "We beg understanding for the ways of our grandfathers," Mr. Tso declared, as if sensing Wilder's weakening rapport. "Our illustrious geomancer is celebrated up and down the river. He was once apprenticed to the great oracle of Amoy. So. Quite so. We are fortunate he is one of our families and can guide us in our escape."

Great, Wilder thought. Splendid.

Dr. Sing sat clutching the soiled bag and the dog-eared book in his lap, and drank his tea noisily. "This humble one wishes only to be of service."

There was the inevitable preliminary small talk. Wilder learned that in addition to his mystic duties, Dr. Sing was also the village letter writer, scroll maker, and intellectual jack-of-all-trades. There was a swollen pride and jealousy behind those windowpane glasses, Wilder thought. He was threadbare at the sleeves and his vest looked as if he'd been wearing it since the Ming dynasty. His clothes smelled sweetly of the black smoke he used.

"I'm anxious to help in any way possible," Wilder said, concealing his impatience. He realized that Dr. Sing had been staring at him. He disliked the feel of the man's eyes on him.

Well, he distrusted the wind-and-water man on sight, and he was sorry for it. There was enough trouble without wondering if the guy was all trickery. A week from tomorrow! Wang would be traced back to Chiku Shan for sure within that time. Dr. Sing might be a member of one of the escaping families, but the Reds had managed to poison family solidarities, and it guaranteed nothing. Still, the Reds would have nothing but contempt for an old-fashioned devil doctor like Dr. Sing, and perhaps that was guarantee enough.

At worst, Wilder admitted, he would probably be nothing more than a mystic pain in the neck.

With their teacups almost empty, Mr. Tso picked up his comb and got on to the point of the visit. "It is hoped," he said, smiling soothingly, "that since it was the eminent brother's hands that delivered the soldier Wang into the great limit, the eminent brother's hands may best assist in discovering the most favorable time for removing the soldier Wang to another shore."

"Yes. I'm willing to try."

"So. Quite so."

Dr. Sing stirred himself and the whole thing was over in less than a minute. Dr. Sing emptied the chamois sack and eight assorted coins sprinkled onto the table. Wilder, following crisp instructions, picked them up, shook them in his large fist, and flattened his hand on the table. Cathy sat silently watching, and he felt like an utter fool.

Dr. Sing, wisely sizing up his audience, eschewed any mumbo-jumbo. With the impatient air of a man convinced he is only wasting his time, he turned his agate eyes toward the combination of coins. After a superficial study he consulted his yellow-backed book, which obviously equated dates to the almost infinite combinations of heads and tails possible with eight different coins.

His waxy fingernail stopped under a black character in the book.

The date.

"It is written," he said, snapping the book closed, "the soldier Wang cannot be removed before November twenty-three."

"Seven months to wait!" Mr. Tso exploded. "*Ai-yu!* We will observe the earlier horoscope."

Wilder had failed.

They left.

Chapter Nine

Wilder was grimly amused. He sat on a straight-backed chair, a towel thrown across his shoulders, and Susu flitted heavily around him with the scissors squeaking in the shuttered bedroom.

"My boilum muchee watah," the amah said. "Captain sailor-man have ploppa bath, you bet."

"Splendid." He'd wait until the village had gone to bed. There wouldn't be much to it. He could handle one of the small junks in the lagoon and there'd be no traffic on the river late at night. He'd dump Wang as near Amoy as he could safely get, and that would be the end of it.

"Captain sailor-man have beforetime piecee wife?"

"What?"

"Mellied?"

"No."

"Velly good."

The amah tipped his head in her quick hands and the squeaking of the scissors resumed. Wilder had been outwitted by eight stupid coins, and he felt reasonably amused now. Dr. Sing had rigged the horoscope; he felt sure of it. A hell of a lot eight coins had to do with getting rid of a dead body, and never mind the occupied coffins awaiting their dates in the temple. Dr. Sing's dirty fingernail could have stopped under any date in the book and no one could have questioned it. The wind-and-water man had come to save face and Wilder couldn't help admiring his cold-blooded arrogance. Mr. Tso had questioned the first divined date and Dr. Sing's power and prestige were challenged. Well, the coins had settled *that*.

"You likee Missy Cathy?"

"Look," Wilder said. "Savee hair on top—understand?"

"My savvy. Savee littee bit, oll ligh."

It would be pleasant, Wilder thought, to break the doctor of magic's neck. He had more pride than sense; the last thing Chiku Shan needed was someone snooping into Wang's whereabouts. Even eight days, by the first horoscope, was too long to wait. The Reds, if Wilder understood them at all, would rather find a soldier dead than missing. If he were missing, there was always the chance he had slipped off for freedom, which was very offensive. If he were found stabbed, it might be taken as something over a woman and of no serious consequence.

Tonight.

Susu stepped back to examine her work, her wide cheekbones gleaming. "Plenty nice job, you bet."

She got back to work and, with his decision firmly made, Wilder thought more tolerantly of the little rooster of a fortuneteller. The guy was as out of date under the Reds as any foreign devil of a China skipper. He was fighting to hold his place under the village sun and perhaps Wilder shouldn't be too crusty with him. His sun, like Wilder's, had set long ago.

Susu was chattering briskly. "Missy Cathy, she likee captain sailor-man. *Yih!* My tinky so!"

"That's swell."

"What ting you tinky 'bout Missy Cathy?"

"I like her," he said. "I think she's swell, and your scissors need oil."

"You bet! My belongee Missy Cathy since mamma die, before time in Peking. Girlee getting old now, needing husband-man. She makee piecee damn fine wife!"

What the hell, Wilder glowered, you scratch an amah and you find a matchmaker. Cathy was fine. Cathy was swell. He'd said that, and he'd meant it, but he wasn't interested in piecee damn fine wife.

"You likee?" Susu bubbled over. "My fixee! My fetchee joss-pidgin-man!"

"Back up." Wilder was impressed with Susu's earnest enthusiasm, and decided to put a quick end to any intrigue on behalf of the God-business-man, the minister. He pursed his lips, caught her wrist, and put an extravagant tenderness into his voice. "Are you blind, Susu? Put down the scissors. Don't you see it's you that has caught the captain sailor-man's eye?"

He pulled her to his lap, and her silken eyebrows swooped. "You clazy!"

"I'm crazy about you. Come close to me, teeth white, lips red."

"*Ai!* My tinky heh all cuttee!"

"Give me a kiss."

She slapped his scalp with the flat of the scissors and jumped up. "You clazy, clazy! Fulla ginger!"

The door slammed.

He laughed.

He carried his own water and bathed in a portable tub made of bamboo and pigskins. He had begun to feel human again. There was no point in worrying about the stern-wheeler. If it had been completely wrecked, that was that, and they'd have to find something else. It might take weeks or months and he preferred not to think about being cooped up in the house for a long wait. At least tonight he had something positive to do. He was responsible for the Wang mess, and he'd clean it up his own way.

He was still in the tub when he heard Koxinga barking in the hall and then Cathy at the door.

"It's me," she said breathlessly. "Can I come in?"

"I wouldn't recommend it," Wilder said. "I'm full of ginger and I'm also in the bathtub."

"There's news. Mr. Tso's nephew has come home—the engineer."

"Good or bad?" he asked crisply.

"The ferry's still afloat," she shouted. "All that happened—they blew a boiler or something trying to get out of the way of the storm. Isn't that wonderful?"

"I'll be right out."

"He says it'll only take a week or so to repair the damage and patch up the ship!"

Wilder tried to get out of the tub without tipping it over.

"Splendid," he said.

Wilder spent an hour with the engineer; who hadn't been able to get any sleep since the typhoon. He was a burly, Westernized Chinese named Tack, with grease-framed fingernails, an Amoy newspaper sticking out of his pocket, and an earthy laugh. He had a fine, shiny nose and apricot eyes. Tack had been trained in the States during the war, and it didn't take Wilder long to discover that the man knew his marine engineering, despite his bursts of rusty English. He had, he explained, blown the old iron boiler purposely after deciding it wouldn't hold up for their hard voyage to Hong Kong. The wine sack of a captain had kept demanding more steam, and, seeing his opportunity, Tack had given it to him. Now they would have a new steel boiler from the repair yards in Amoy, and never mind if this delay upset Dr. Sing's calculations. Tack admitted frankly that his branch of the Tso family had been rice Christians for a brief spell, and were, if nothing else, disenchanted with *Fêng-Shui*—at least when it got in the way.

"What about an engineering gang on this voyage of ours?" Wilder asked.

Tack's eyes took on a gleam of malicious humor. "Aye,

Captain, I fix. One of my wipers good man, I trust, he go with us to Hong Kong, O.K.? I make him assistant engineer. Other men I train from the village, firemen, wipers, many months now. Aye, Captain. One at a time they come aboard, I tell Captain they want to learn, he make a little squeeze, but O.K.—they learn plenty. All trained now. Set."

Wilder wasn't concerned about a deck gang; the village junkmen would know enough to tie up and cast off. Before Tack left for his family and his bed, Wilder got his first technical information on this ship he was to command. She had a low-pressure engine that could turn out eight knots with a wind behind her. She was 110 tons and drew fourteen inches of water, which was more than Wilder had given her flat bottom. The gauges were all accomplished liars, the steam lines were always clogging, and one of the buckets on the paddle wheel was missing. She was old enough to be anyone's grandmother, but there was another three hundred miles in her anyway, and Hong Kong was little farther.

"Aye, Captain," the engineer said smartly. "She's a fine ship."

Cathy, a green velvet ribbon in her hair, was silent through dinner, and Susu served him brusquely. They ate some bony river fish that kept them reasonably busy and made the silence tolerable. In brief glances, Wilder studied Cathy's mood, and decided not to force a conversation. It was her father, he thought. This was the night he expected the ferry to leave, and that made him overdue. The Fengs had come home, the engineer had come home, but not Dr. Grainger, and she was beginning to worry. What was keeping him in Swatow? The large plastered dining room, lit with bean-oil lamps, seemed cold and empty, and Wilder was glad to get the meal over with.

"I guess I'll get busy on my chart," he said, getting up. There was still Wang to be got out of their hair; the week or so it would take to get the ferry operating again had changed nothing.

Cathy looked up. "Do you suppose something's happened to Dad?"

"He'll show up. He's not the first man to be late for dinner."

"He'd have got back today if he could."

"You're not doing yourself any good, Cathy. Maybe the coaster had a breakdown. Maybe anything. Swatow's a long way down the coast, and even the Reds haven't been able to make things run on time."

She smiled a little and let it go.

He stood around for another moment, but when she didn't pick up the conversation he started for the stairway. Hell, he thought, I'm rotten at tender little situations like this. He was sorry for her, but there was really nothing he could do.

He turned at the foot of the stairs. "Is the village gate kept locked at night?"

Her eyebrows lifted with quick suspicion. "Yes."

"I thought I heard a night watchman's rattle last night. Did I?"

"Yes."

Then there was a village *ta-keng-ti* he'd have to avoid. And he'd need something to manage the wall with. He supposed a rope was too much to hope for. Well, he'd figure out something. "Thanks."

He got out his chart and had barely started another session on it when he discovered Cathy in the bedroom with him.

"If you're going somewhere, I'm going with you."

The flaming pith wicks in the old-fashioned saucer lamps sent their shadows flickering across the bed.

"Relax," he said. "I'm not running out."

"It's Wang, isn't it?"

"That's right."

"I can help."

"I can manage it alone."

Her eyes were bright and earnest. "Let me go—*please*."

He stared at her for a moment. Maybe that's what she needed too, something to be doing. "Suit yourself," he said. "I'll get changed."

"There's plenty of time."

Peering through the shutters, he saw a square lantern on the move below. The watchman had come round again, shaking his wooden rattle to signal the time. The eleven-to-one-o'clock watch had begun: three shakes on the rattle every few paces. Now was as good a time as any to get started, Wilder decided.

He picked up the leather rope he'd made out of the portable bathtub, slicing it into strips with Wang's bayonet. He'd sent the amah for the newspaper he'd seen sticking out of Tack's pocket, and put it now in his own. It would be useful in the plan that had taken shape in his mind.

Cathy was waiting in a wadded cotton jacket, her hair tucked into a tam. She looked older somehow, strikingly beautiful in coolie garb, and entirely calm.

"You'll be cold," she said. "I got one of Dad's sweaters for you."

He slipped it on, a black turtle-neck affair, and they parted in the lane outside the compound. She took the rope; he'd meet her somewhere along the village wall, north of the gate.

The *ta-keng-ti's* wooden rattle sounded far off. The moon hadn't yet risen; clouds hovered over the village and the river and a night breeze carried with it the tangy, resinous scent of pines.

Wilder hadn't thought to bring any light. The temple door hadn't been fixed and he entered the incense-sweet storeroom quickly. He spent a long time blindly searching for the laundry basket. He never found it. But he discovered Wang's body in the coffin reserved for Wilder.

Rigor mortis had come and gone. With Wang across his shoulder he stopped short in the temple moon gate. The rattle was shaking very near. Finally the glow of the lantern receded and Wilder got under way again.

Cathy was waiting at the wall. It rose at least twenty feet; there was little rope to spare. Once up the broken stone stairs to the parapet, they lowered Wang to make sure the pigskin line would hold, and it did. Cathy worked her way down next, and Wilder followed.

The rest was easy. They untied one of the two small fishing junks and Cathy poled off while Wilder raised the ribbed lugsail. The pulleys squeaked like sea gulls, but the noises went nowhere against the bubbling murmur of the waterfall.

Once they were in the river, the sail caught the wind like a patched fan.

"Can you handle a rudder?" Wilder asked.

"Yes."

He left her with the sweat-worn tiller and moved forward under the mat canopy. There were heavy stones aboard and he wondered again what the village fishermen were up to. He got Tack's newspaper in his hand and rolled Wang over. If the soldier were found with that day's newspaper in his green pocket, it might advance the assumed date of his death. Chiku Shan would be well out of it. Wang would appear to have been killed the day *after* the village search.

He covered Wang with some nets as they met a flat-nosed sampan coming from the city with night soil. Finally he worked his way aft again.

"I'll take it."

But she didn't give up the rudder and the water went whispering under them. She tacked past a lamplit crew of rivermen floating logs toward Amoy and Wilder was impressed. The April night had come down with a chill and her face was bright with the cold. They rode high over the water on the creaking arched stern, and Wilder began to relax.

"There's a lot of granite aboard," Wilder said. "Where does it go?"

Cathy's voice was maliciously enigmatic. "They're building up a couple of spots in the river—one in the estuary and one outside the lagoon. It's been going on secretly for months now, a few stones at a time, so no one will pay any attention to it."

"I see." He didn't see, but he let it go. He was glad Cathy had come along. He liked the look of the tiller in her long fingers where gnarled brown hands belonged. She appeared to know this north branch of the Dragon River and steered audaciously. Susu's canary-like voice went fluttering through his mind again: "She makee piecee damn fine wife!"

"You can't see anything now," she said, "but we're passing a deserted village. There are several scattered along the river."

"Wiped out by the Reds?"

"Wiped out by tea. They're sort of like the ghost towns of your West. When the tea trade died around here, a lot of the villages emptied. Surely you know the oolong your Indians dumped into Boston Harbor came out of Amoy?"

"Cut it out," he muttered. In the old days that was the first thing they told you in any Amoy teahouse or gambling joint when they recognized you for an American, as if the Fukien tea planters had all but won your Revolutionary War.

They were approaching the islands where the north and south forks of the river met, and Wilder made a sudden change of plan. There was no point in tempting fate by turning left for Amoy and beaching Wang somewhere near the island. The moon was up now and the charcoal clouds looked swollen with rain. Better get it over with, he thought, and get out.

"Hard over," he said, putting his hand on the tiller.

Cathy put all her weight against it, and once through a tight group of islands in the estuary, they entered the South River.

"Going to Changchow?" Cathy muttered.

"Not that far."

The river hills had fallen away into alluvial flats and Wilder felt more exposed. He took over the rudder and after a dark mile or two pulled in toward shore.

This was far enough.

With Wang once more hoisted to his shoulder, he waded across an oyster bed and propped the comrade on slightly higher ground. It was as much as he could think to do. Wang would be found with that day's newspaper in his pocket and along the South River. Chiku Shan, on the North River, shouldn't even cross their minds.

He got back to the junk and washed his hands in the tide.

The clouds burst before they found their way back to their own fork of the river.

"Get under the canopy," Wilder said. "I'll take the tiller."

"I don't mind getting wet."

"You're crazy."

He found a stiff oilskin and threw it across her

shoulders. The wind changed and the rudder bobbed in its rope tackles. Wilder busied himself with the sail and the rain pelted down in large, stinging drops. When he returned to Cathy, only her oval face showed under the oilskin, and the rain rattled against it like buckshot.

"You're a pretty good sailor," he said.

"Thanks."

"Where'd you learn?"

"What?"

"Keep your eye on the road."

The junk seemed a ton lighter without Wang aboard. Even Cathy feels it, he thought. She's sitting there as if she owns the goddamned river now. She's happy as hell. "He'll never forgive you for this," Cathy shouted.

"What?"

"Dr. Sing."

"He'll never know for sure. Let him wonder."

He could see the glint of her teeth through the rain. *Ch'ih-pai-ch'un*, he thought. Teeth white, lips red—beautiful. Beautiful and strange. "Missy Cathy, she likee captain sailor-man. *Yih!* My tinky so!" Wilder shrugged off his thoughts. Make a pass at her and the poor kid would start shopping for peach blossoms.

"Where'd you learn?" he shouted again.

"I've handled Dad's junk. That's how he makes his calls. It's fixed up like a one-room hospital."

"I see."

"Did you notice my bed? It came out of the junk."

"I'll be damned."

"I mean—well, there used to be a quack doctor who worked the river. Not a doctor, really. He more or less guaranteed male heirs."

"Say on."

"I suppose you'd call it a racket." The downpour lost its first impact, softening, and her voice dropped.

"Anyway, too many girl babies came along and he lost face. Dad bought his junk and I got the bed. You must admit it's a beautiful bit of furniture."

"Sure. Now will you explain what the devil you're talking about?"

"Look." She paused uneasily, apparently sorry she'd brought the matter up. "You see, it's a celestial bed. Magic. If you needed a male baby to continue your line, you—just rented the junk for the night."

"Steady as you go."

Chapter Ten

Communist posters had been plastered along the village wall, bright and new and arrogant in the sun. Old Feng had brought them from Changchow and now you had to look past Chairman Mao's ice-water grin any time you glanced at the river.

Every morning Wilder amused himself at the slats of his shutters as the Red elder took his day's exercise. There'd be the safari across the courtyard with grandsons or nephews on hand to help the aching bulk into the shell of the Rolls-Royce brought from the Philippines. At various times during the day Wilder watched figures come and go, and if the wind was right he could hear the tinkle of the small bell that apparently meant Grandfather Feng was in need of something.

The old bastard, Wilder thought, he'd split a gut if he knew there was an American watching him.

Wilder had brought his chart as far as he could. There was nothing left to do but wait. The villagers had made him a pair of thick-soled leather sandals, chuckling over their size, and two pajama-like suits made of blue cotton. He felt like a Shantung ricksha puller.

When more than a week had passed he became impossibly restless and one night he and Cathy went for a swim in the lagoon. Cathy no longer mentioned her father. Whatever her feelings, she covered them with a thin veneer of brightness. She was fun. But if there was no sign of worry on her face, it appeared on Wilder's. He felt that he knew her less and less each day, and it bothered him.

Wilder was gradually briefed on all the long-planned details of the escape. He learned of the false ferryboat funnel made by Li the village carpenter and Li the village metalworker. It had long been finished and painted to imitate the stack of the paddle-wheeler, and waited in a cave above the lagoon for the night they would steal the ship. Dr. Sing explained confidently that the gods had changed their minds and blown the iron boiler to prevent an ill-fated voyage. A new departure date had been calculated, and on April 18, eleven days after the typhoon, word came that the ferry was back on its run, shuttling passengers between Amoy, Kulangsu, and the mainland.

But still they waited, and still the two small fishing junks left the lagoon with their cargoes of stones.

Each day brought its own weather and Wilder cursed this Chinese April and the exasperating ways of the village. A fog had come in on April 20, drifting through the pines and blotting out the river, but Chiku Shan sat patiently through it. The wind-and-water man had petitioned the spirits and the spirits advised April 23 for the piracy and April 26 for the start of the voyage itself. It was absurd.

But it was written.

"Six more days to wait." Wilder smiled wearily at dinner under the flickering bean-oil lamps. "What a splendid bunch of nonsense!" He found some grim humor in the stalemated situation. One little rooster of a man had stopped the escape machinery cold, and you had to admire the guy's cold nerve even though you wanted to wrap the zodiac around his scrawny neck. "It's also written that a lost inch of gold may be found, but a lost inch of time—never."

"Susu made *san-fan* just for you tonight." Cathy passed the plate. "Because she knows you don't like them."

He ignored the fried flour cakes. "I'll explain," he said elaborately. "There's this big white thing that lives in the sky. It's called the moon."

"I know. You've never been able to see the old man chopping down the tree and it's marked you for life."

"It rises fifty-one minutes later every day—even in China. I've watched it. It really happens that way."

"Quaint."

"Very quaint. Now this morning it came up just after dawn. The longer we wait, the later the moon's going to stick in the night sky, and the more exposed we'll be thrashing down the coast. Clear?"

"Perfectly."

"No," he said. "The answer is so, quite so." He'd felt like a fool arguing the matter with the old man. The *ti-pao* could do nothing but smile his wrinkled brown smile. The eminent brother knew best these things of the physical world, true, but the underworld too must be judged, and this was the province, of the gifted *Fêng-Shui* doctor. Dr. Sing had reckoned the harmonious times, when the earth currents of the dragon and the tiger would be in balance, and even the village elder was powerless to complain. His people would refuse to board the ferryboat a moment sooner, for the evil spirits would be released to plague them and the voyage would surely end in disaster. So. Quite so.

"I admit it." Cathy smiled honestly. "Dr. Sing is a nuisance. But really, he did his celestial best. More tea?"

"We don't know that he looks up the right pages in his grimy almanac books."

"It can't make too much difference."

"Funny," he said. "I thought I just finished a lecture on that."

"Oh, yes. The big white thing that lives in the sky."

"More tea." He shrugged.

Well, Dr. Sing had flexed his fortunetelling muscles and there was nothing to do but drink tea, Wilder thought. Nothing had come of the Wang mess, but Wilder wondered if the village was paying the price of violating Dr. Sing's first untouchable advice. Wilder couldn't pirate the ferry alone and now the little man in the dirty vest was showing his full power and arrogance.

Susu brought in a fresh pot of tea and set it noisily on the tile. "'Melican ollo time hully-up. Hully-up. Chop-chop. No good. Plenty time, you bet, plenty time."

It was a moment before Wilder realized that the amah had been trying to tell him something. He glanced at Cathy and it penetrated. They had begun to pull in different directions, and he'd been entirely blind to it. She was dreading the day they'd leave the village. Every day they were delayed meant one more day when Dr. Grainger might walk in the door.

That night they let themselves over the wall with the leather line and went swimming. The water was icy and the stars stood bright and close over the lagoon. Cathy kept a whispered gaiety going between them until finally her teeth began to chatter, and they pulled out of the water onto one of the junks. He had never seen her in higher spirits and it made him slightly uneasy. She seemed to have made up her mind not to discuss her father with him, but he felt the things that were being left unsaid.

"If your teeth don't stop chattering the watchman's going to hear us down here."

"Let him."

He wrapped a blanket around her and she pulled off her bathing cap.

"Tom?"

"I'm hungry. Next time let's pack a lunch."

"You've never tried to kiss me."

"Haven't I?"

"You've been busy, I guess."

"Yes."

"But it is rather maddening. I mean, wondering if you're ever going to try."

"I can't imagine anything less enticing than a pair of chattering lips."

"They've stopped. See?"

He lifted her chin with his wet knuckles and kissed her. He felt her arms slip around his shoulders and his temples began to pound. That was as far as he let it go. He broke her embrace and got back to his feet. Let's not spoil it, baby, he thought. You'll make someone piecee damn fine wife, but not me. I like being with you, I like eating with you, I like swimming with you, but I don't want to make a fool of you. Clear? Once we reach Hong Kong you'll never see me again. Didn't I tell you? "Let's go."

"*Ai-tsai!*" Cathy frowned sadly. "He kisses like a gust of wind."

Once over the wall, Wilder coiled the leather and slung it over his shoulder. He felt entirely ridiculous and was glad when they reached the house. He supposed she was laughing at him. Did she think he was afraid of her? He wished now he could play the scene over again. Why had he given a damn? She was nothing to him, just a fetching English girl who happened to live in the village. Cathy had known what she was up to on the junk. Where had his phantom of a conscience come from? She slept every night in a celestial bed made for two and perhaps imagination had caught up with her. What was he waiting for, Dr. Sing to reckon the harmonious time for vagrant lovemaking? Cathy hadn't been dewy-eyed about the matter and he had been a fool.

They let themselves into the house and Wilder lit a lamp in the living room. Cathy's hair had got wet around the golden edges and the night air had left a lovely brightness in her eyes.

"Don't go, Cathy."

Her shadow stopped along the plaster wall. There was something faintly reviling in her smile. He was, after all, an absurdity, and she had misjudged him.

"I suppose," Wilder said, "Susu warned you about me."

"She's put a hand bell beside my bed. All I have to do is ring it and she'll come running."

"Would you?"

"I wouldn't have. I think I would now."

"Good night, Cathy."

"Don't think—" She stopped herself and went up the stairs. She was a good deal more scared than she would ever admit, he thought. He doubted that she had ever held a man in her arms before. She had probably coolly decided she wanted to try, and that had been the end of any debate in her mind. He wondered if he'd find her sitting up in bed with the bell clutched in her hands. Her pride was aroused now and he supposed he was wasting his time.

He killed the light finally and went upstairs. He

opened the door to his own bedroom to drop off the scaling rope, and almost at once the odor of cigarette smoke stopped him. He saw a pink coal near the shutters. A voice came softly.

"Ah, Captain Wilder?"

He struck a match and saw Mr. Tso sitting in the chair at the window. His eyes were heavy and there was no smile hanging from them in the wrinkles. Wilder carried the match to a lamp.

"Come right in," he said.

"You must forgive this intrusion. I wished to speak to you alone. I have waited over an hour, but it is nothing."

"I suppose you're wondering where I've been."

"That is not my affair. I found the outer door unlocked and the house dark. It is not my way to enter uninvited, but it seemed wise on this occasion. I came directly to this room and contented myself to wait."

Wilder thought of Cathy in the bedroom down the hall and wished the old man would get on with it. Couldn't it have waited until morning? "I regret that I kept you waiting."

"To explain—my unworthy nephew who calls himself Tack brought the Amoy newspaper tonight. It contains news of our Dr. Grainger."

Wilder's attention sharpened. The drawn look on Mr. Tso's great face suggested the headline. "Go on."

"It is as we secretly feared. So. It appears that a certain general died under Dr. Grainger's unsteady knife. His knife often swims in rice wine, I regret. He was accused of murder and sentenced to death by a People's court in Swatow. The sentence has been carried out."

Wilder was silent.

"Unfortunate," Mr. Tso said. "He was a very good

BLOOD ALLEY 97

man and all of us have our weaknesses. But it is Miss Grainger that concerns us. With my people, death is—expected. She has no one else in the world, and I come to you for advice. I do not pretend to understand the mind of your people. Perhaps you will know best how to prepare her for this unhappy news."

"You're asking me to tell her?"

"Perhaps you would agree."

Wilder wanted to protest, but Mr. Tso was already rising and he saw it would be no use. The village would wait for the American to break the news. It was proper.

A moment later Mr. Tso left the house. Wilder sat on the edge of his bed, weary and just slightly angry. The last thing he cared to tell Cathy was that her father had been butchered by a bunch of Swatow Reds.

Well, he couldn't go down the hall now, not with Cathy waiting there with or without the bell in her hands. It would be completely cruel.

He undressed finally, felt his way to his brass bed, and tried to get some sleep.

Chapter Eleven

The first of the fishing junks set out through the ancient darkness just after twilight. Wilder, garbed in the homespun robe and hood of a Buddhist monk, found a spot for himself at the bow. He wore a string of porcelain prayer beads around his neck and he carried the Tokarev automatic tucked in the belt of his blue trousers underneath.

April twenty-third had come.

The other junk, towing a long raft piled high with pine faggots, would follow down the river an hour later. The raft was already being prepared in the lagoon, and Wilder glimpsed the dummy ship's funnel that had been brought out of hiding in the cave. It had the flared crown and black stovepipe length he had seen often enough from Kulangsu as the paddle-wheeler churned in and out of the harbor. The cousins Li had made a convincing copy and the twigs would conceal it on the raft.

Wilder felt a sense of release and even a strange sense of destiny; he'd felt it the moment they poled off. The junk was crowded and noisy—there were eleven of them in the raiding party—and he enjoyed the noise. Every flat face shone in the darkness; the waiting of many months was over. *Hao!* Now the stupid Feng clan is a prisoner in its own house. Did you hear the old rice sack of an elder wail? A pity we must take them with us to Hong Kong. Would they do as much for us? Tonight the fire-wheel boat is ours, cousins! *Ai*, tonight we show the Red pigs what our grandfathers taught the Manchus in their day!

Tonight, Wilder reminded himself, an old wound would begin to heal.

He pushed the hood back off his head and gazed at the bent shadows grouped under the canopy and sitting on the damp nets. He listened and grinned slightly. Despite his enthusiasm for the business at hand, he felt outside the camaraderie that rolled through the junk. They chattered of pirate ancestors and their pistols clicked as they checked over the parts again. Like the false smokestack, Chiku Shan's armory had come out of hiding—a pawnshop collection left by old armies. He caught glints of Japanese Nambus and American Colts. If all went as planned, no one would have to fire a shot.

It had rained late in the afternoon; the river air was now still and muggy. Once they were out of the lagoon, the sail was hoisted, and Big Han, who commanded the group, asked for silence. Voices carry far on a night like this, cousins.

The moon still lagged, as if caught in the treetops across the river, but the mouth of the river would be pitch-dark by the time they reached it, and to Wilder that was all that mattered.

Wilder glanced behind to Chiku Shan, sitting high in the gloom like something built by a vanished race of giants. He thought of Cathy. How had two days passed without his telling her, he wondered? Somehow the right moment hadn't come along. Or if it had, perhaps he'd let it pass. When *was* the right moment to tell someone there had been a sort of murder in the family? Well, he'd kept putting it off and she was still waiting for Dr. Grainger to walk in the door and the last days had been pretty damned uncomfortable. He couldn't bring himself to watch her get hurt, but after two days the situation was absurd. He was puzzled by his own lack of courage.

"You are comfortable, *ch'uan-chang?*"

Wilder looked up from his wrists and saw that Big Han had come forward in the junk. Size is relative. Big Han barely came to Wilder's shoulder, but he had a broad, stocky build and a large, glistening, amiable face.

"I'm steaming in this tent of a robe." Wilder grinned.

"The weather cannot make up its mind. Still, you must remember to keep the hood in place once we are in public places. Our monks shave their heads and such things will give you away."

"Sit down."

Big Han nodded his shaggy head toward the others. "You hear? Tonight we are reminded of our grandfathers in the days of Koxinga, and we feel their blood of three centuries ago. They too fought for freedom, even though they were pirates, yes? We prefer not to remember that they lost."

"They'd have won if they'd kept to their ships," Wilder said. "But your fleet went to Peiping and tried to fight like an army."

"It is a pity, yes. And a lesson. Whenever I go to the mouth of the river I remember that once there were eight hundred pirate junks anchored there. It must have been a sight."

"I'd like to have seen it." Wilder knew little of the Han family except that the men were lacquer carvers, growing their own "varnish trees" in wooden tubs, and the sharpness of resin and cinnabar clung to Big Han even now.

"My own distant grandfather served as one of Koxinga's bodyguards," he said, lighting the stub of a cigarette. "The stories are handed down."

"If one could move the stone tiger of six hundred pounds' weight, then he was selected for Koxinga's Tiger Guard. It was a great honor. The Hans have always been strong, but the Tsos are smarter. That too was handed down. We have still my grandfather's iron apron and his arrows with the red and green stripes. But I bore you with my family stories." He grinned sheepishly and got out a folded piece of paper, straightening it across his stocky knee. It was a hand-drawn map of the estuary. In the weak glow of the junk lantern Wilder could make out the two pincers of land gripping the islands scattered in the Dragon's mouth. Outside stood the larger islands of Amoy and Kulangsu. The dotted lines, Wilder assumed, would indicate the usual route of the ferryboat.

"We go aboard as mere passengers here at Shihma," the Chinese said, pointing to a spot on the south shore of the estuary.

"Nine o'clock."

"Yes. Last ferry trip for the night. From Shihma it

stops at Hai-ch'eng, and then sails out across the river mouth to Amoy and Kulangsu. A long trip."

"Yes."

"We take the ship here, just past this island, which will conceal us from the town of Hai-ch'eng. There, too, our cousins will erect the smokestack in the water."

"What about the regular passengers picked up at Shihma and Hai-ch'eng?"

"There should be few on this late trip. We have checked many times. They will be only a small bother, *ch'uan-chang*."

Wilder nodded. Mr. Tso wasn't in the habit of overlooking details. It would go off with precision.

The junk reached the outskirts of Shihma a few minutes after eight-thirty. They separated in groups of two and three and would meet several blocks away at the wharf. Another of Mr. Tso's nephews guided Wilder through the streets, reminding him to walk slowly, as becomes a monk. Other villagers were already at the wharf when Wilder showed up and young Tso moved off to buy tickets. The knots of villagers ignored each other.

Wilder, feeling conspicuous in his monk's robe, stood at the darkest corner of the dock and was glad for the hood. The minutes began to drag. A Hakka woman in a black fringed hat joined the waiting passengers. Beyond the wharf lights the river was black. Wilder kept an ear cocked for the high-pitched ferry whistle and the familiar chunking of its paddle wheel.

"*Mai-pi-tsu-ooo! Mai-pi-tsu-oooooo!*"

The wail of a water chestnut vendor spread along the wharf instead. The old man came under the strand of weak lights where most of the passengers waited and a wide-hipped figure disengaged itself from the others. He stopped the vendor, and Wilder's eyes tightened with recognition. The sale was made, the wail resumed, and Wilder stared.

He'd know that chunky figure anywhere. Black Pigeon.

Black Pigeon, the bribed guard, waiting for the ferry to take him to Kulangsu and his ten-o'clock shift at the jail.

Wilder tugged down sharply on the hood and swore to himself. He sent for Big Han and wondered what Black Pigeon might do if he recognized the escaped American. No one had put gold in his hands to cover this night's operation. It would be his chance to play Red hero.

"*Mai-pi-tsu-ooo!*"

Wilder shook his head and the chestnut vendor passed him by. Black Pigeon wouldn't matter once they were aboard the steamboat. What the hell was keeping it? The guard licked his fingers impatiently and began pacing around. It must be nine, at least, Wilder thought. Was the turtle of a ferryboat going to make Black Pigeon late again?

Big Han wandered over.

"We must be patient," he whispered. "Perhaps there is another breakdown. We will wait until midnight if necessary."

"Have someone tag that little comrade," Wilder muttered. "He's from the jail. He knows me. He might decide to make trouble if he got a look at my face."

Big Han glanced back and nodded with a grin. "We will be prepared to persuade him otherwise. But his type cannot look a monk in the face."

During the next moments Wilder watched the villagers take new positions closer to Black Pigeon, and he tried to relax. But any incident on the wharf at this stage of the operation would be a nightmare.

Half an hour later they heard the distant throb of the paddle wheel somewhere below them on the Nan

Chiang, and finally the breathless little ship's whistle.

Before the night was over Wilder ought to be master of a ship again.

Chapter Twelve

She kicked up a cloud of spray in the night.

Under the string of wharf lights her brown skin looked rusty and streaked and her narrow hips were festooned with worn-out automobile tires, serving for bumpers. Her tall black funnel belched smoke that blotted out the stars and rained cinders on the waiting passengers. The bumpers squealed against the wharf and lines were thrown out. Her boiler deck was badly lit and partly open; above it the stained-glass windows of the saloon looked like fugitives from the Gay Nineties. She rose still higher in the air with a texas deck of first-class cabins, and despite the corseting of hog frames and a hog-post, her weather deck was swaybacked. Above it all, rubbing its back against the chimney, sat the dark box of the pilothouse. Her guardrails and bulkheads dripped gingerbread; she was tall and skinny and foolish-looking.

Gazing at her at close quarters for the first time, Wilder wondered if it was all madness. Whatever majesty she might once have had was reduced to sags and broken windows and bailing wire. Her face hadn't been washed in years, and she smelled of perspiration.

Wilder was one of the last to go aboard.

He saw Black Pigeon head for the lighted saloon and decided to stay out of it. Once he felt the wood of a ship's deck under his feet, Wilder's sudden depression left him. He picked up the skirt of his robe and went up the ladder to the hurricane deck. He glanced again at the black glass windows of the pilothouse and his enthusiasm returned. Whatever she looked like, she was afloat, and she had an engine and a paddle wheel to push her. That was all that really mattered.

Under the dirty stars crates of vegetables from the truck farms around Shihma were shuffled aboard and Wilder took the delay patiently. Chiku Shan would be eating fresh lettuce and onions, sweet potatoes and sugar cane all the way to Hong Kong.

Bells clattered in the pilothouse and a moment later the stern wheel dug in and the crowned funnel erupted smoke and sparks. The ferry came around for the return trip to Amoy. Once out of the wharf lights, Wilder felt his way through the guy wires to the lure of the open engine-room hatch. He moved forward and peered down at the machined bowels of the ship. The pungent warmth of lubricating oil came to his nostrils, sweet and delicious. The glints of steel and brass met his eyes and he saw that Tack kept a spotless world down there, as if he loved every wrench and cam like a Scotchman. Wilder found himself a box to sit on and waited out the lights of Hai-ch'eng.

The ferry made its last mainland stop and half a dozen passengers came aboard. Big Han and young Tso appeared on the weather deck and approached Wilder.

"All is in readiness," Big Han muttered warmly. "Cousin Tack sends his apologies for the delay in reaching Shihma. He demanded more wood be taken aboard in Amoy in order that the fuel boxes be full for our journey."

"He'll steal them blind if he has the chance."

It had been a disappointment to Wilder when Tack had informed him that the steamer burned wood. Tack promised he would do his noisy best to wrangle coal these last few days, although he had little hope of it.

Coal was too expensive and scarce to be issued to this river-going stove. On their voyage they would have to be content, he feared, with the space problem of a wood cargo, as in the past.

"Now we have only to wait, *ch'uan-chang*," Big Han said.

The two men joined Wilder on boxes and smoked cigarettes. The captain kept a dirty ship and Wilder was already thinking of things to be done once the paddle-wheeler was tied up in the lagoon. The top deck had a miserable sag and he would see if the guys radiating from the center hog post could be tightened up. He wondered if there was a bucket of paint anywhere in the ship's locker. There certainly had never been a mop.

The whistle puffed.

"All right," Wilder said gently. "Once the fire starts, I'll rush the wheelhouse from starboard. You two come in on the port side—that side there. It's a hot night and the doors are wide open."

"Yes, it won't be necessary to knock, *ch'uan-chang*."

"Don't pull your trigger unless there's more trouble than we can handle. And if you've got to, don't shoot me. It's dark in there. The pilot can see better. No glare."

"A few moments and it should begin."

The lights of Hai-ch'eng blinked out behind the shoulder of an island. The minutes began to tighten up. Tack, he knew, had planted three homemade smoke bombs in the engine room and the wiper would set them off. The fiddley door in the saloon had been propped wide open and you could always count on passengers standing around to watch the gleaming stroke of the giant piston. Smoke would pour out into their faces to convince them the ship was on fire, and they'd carry the tale ashore with them. It was a vital detail.

Wilder finally came out from under his hood and the three of them got out their guns.

And then Black Pigeon came clattering up the ladder to the hurricane deck.

At the same moment the rectangle of light from the engine-room hatch turned white. The smoke had started.

"*Huo!*"

It was a lone wail from the deck below. One of the villagers, Wilder knew, stirring up the alarm. Big Han started forward, but Wilder put out a hand to stop him.

"Wait."

"I can put a knife in the pig of a guard."

"Hold on, cousin."

Smoke began to trail the ferry in paper-white streamers and the alarm spread like a disease from voice to voice. Black Pigeon froze in flat-footed amazement in the companionway. He gazed wide-eyed at the smoke boiling out of the engine-room hatch. The clatter of running feet below mixed with the confusion of voices.

"We sink! *Huo! Lifeboats!* Fire! Fire!"

Black Pigeon turned white and went slipping down the ladder.

"All right," Wilder said. "Let's take the pilothouse."

They spread across the deck and a mad exchange of bells cut through the smoke. Tack was raising hell over his primitive engine room telegraph. Approaching the wheelhouse, Wilder heard a stormy Chinese voice trying to make itself heard through the voice tube. The captain.

Poor bastard, Wilder thought.

When he reached the starboard doorway a chest full of gold buttons rushed directly into Wilder's gun.

"*Ch'ieh-chu!*" Wilder said crisply. "Now back up, Captain. You're not going anywhere. This is a gun in your belly."

"*Ai!*"

The captain had received a gift of whisky from his chief engineer that afternoon; Wilder now got the full blast of his inflammable breath.

"Quickly!"

The captain spread his pudgy hands and backed into the pilothouse. Big Han and his cousins were already removing the steersman from the wheel. The white smoke, the terrified yelling below, and a huge monk with a hard gun in his hand reduced the captain to a breathless babble. It wasn't a moment Wilder cared to remember.

"*Kun-pa! Kun-pa!* Who—what—"

Wilder grabbed the gold-freckled captain by his lapels and pulled him to the voice pipes.

"Abandon ship! Yell it down the tubes!"

"*Kun-pa! Kun-pa!*"

"Yell it!" Wilder knew every inch of the pilothouse from Tack's diagram; he reached overhead and gave five short jerks on the whistle cord. Abandon ship. But it was a question, Tack warned, whether the birdbrained deck crew knew the ferry's signals.

The captain began to mutter into the tubes.

"Louder!"

"Yes, yes, abandon ship. Engine room! Boiler room!"

They'd know the captain's voice squeaking down there, and all but Tack and the wiper would clear out; once the lifeboats had shoved off, the villagers Tack had trained would take up their engine-room stations and start feeding the furnace.

"All right," Wilder snapped. "Well done, Captain." He found the megaphone. "Now out on deck. *K'uai-k'uai!*"

Big Han took over on the whistle and kept it

coughing. Wilder bent the captain over the rail, the gun in his ample back and the megaphone at his lips. Smoke was drifting out of the broken saloon windows and a nice confusion was sweeping the decks.

"Let them hear it in Amoy," Wilder growled. "Lifeboats! Abandon ship!"

The *ch'uan-chang* came out of his alcoholic daze long enough to attempt a show of self-respect, and balked.

"Yell it!"

Wilder shoved the gun harder in his back and a burst of sour breath escaped the megaphone. Villagers were already swinging out two lifeboats and Wilder saw that Black Pigeon was one of the first aboard.

The deck crew wasn't waiting for the captain's order.

Some twenty minutes later the two boats could be seen drifting aft, and young Tso informed Wilder, with an ear-to-ear grin, that they were now alone on the ship.

The steersman and the captain were made prisoners in the captain's own cabin and Wilder took the wheel in his sweaty hands. One of the village junkmen took up his position at the windows to pilot Wilder through the shallows of the river.

Wilder missed the engine-order telegraph. The pilothouse was linked to the engine room by bell cords and voice tubes, and he'd have to get used to it.

Wilder pressed his lips to one of the tubes. "Chief engineer!"

"Aye, Captain!"

"It's a fine night."

"Welcome aboard, Captain!"

"I'm having the Red flag taken down from the jack staff."

"Send it down. We make steam of it."

"Let's go home."

"Aye, Captain!"

Wilder had the ship completely darkened and clanged the bell for slow speed ahead. The engine began to rumble and the piston slipped into its stroke. The paddle wheel creaked and splashed and the ferryboat began to move.

The lifeboats had vanished in the darkness toward Hai-ch'eng. Tomorrow they would tell the story of the great fire. With the wheel spokes in his hands, Wilder once more felt in his element. He squared his shoulders and he was grinning like everyone else aboard. They had pirated the boat, China fashion, and it had gone smoothly.

Big Han re-entered the wheelhouse and assured Wilder that the ship was completely dark. He cupped a flashlight over his hand-drawn map of the estuary and pointed to the spot where the other village crew was planting the dummy ship's funnel.

"I'll do my best not to hit it." Wilder smiled.

They were working, as well as he could figure, somewhere in the darkness to starboard.

"Put a lookout at the bow in case we've drifted too far out."

"It has already been done, *ch'uan-chang*. It would be a pity if we crushed their work, eh?"

The rudder responded sluggishly. Wilder would have to learn to anticipate. There was nothing but stars and river blackness outside the pilothouse windows. He would have liked to see the work of the other village crew. The phony chimney was being fixed in place on a submerged pile of rocks at a depth of five fathoms. For months the junks had been dropping granite boulders while pretending to fish the area, and Wilder found himself taking some pleasure in Chinese patience. Tomorrow four feet of smokestack would stand out of muddy water to convince anyone that the stern-wheeler had burned and gone to the bottom. It wasn't likely that anyone would be interested in refloating the tottering old ship—and discover nothing but a giant stovepipe set in a pile of rocks.

With the junkman calling out warnings, Wilder picked his way through the islands to the Pei Chiang and then into the north branch of the Dragon River. He crept along at half speed in order to keep sparks and the funnel glow down.

"We're being seen," Wilder said, glancing toward Big Han. "There are sampans in the river."

Big Han seemed unconcerned. "Yes. But our Red masters have not learned to hold two opposite thoughts in their heads at once. A few river coolies may claim they saw the ferry in the river, and they will be laughed at. Didn't the very passengers see it burn? And to save face the crew will insist it sank. Look! The chimney still sits there in the water like a gravestone!"

Chapter Thirteen

It was past midnight when the stern-wheeler left the river for the narrow channel just north of the Chiku Shan bluff and entered the lagoon. Wilder felt as if he were sailing into a bottle.

There were hand lanterns swinging along the stone landing and plenty of hands to grab the lines. After another moment Wilder rang below to stop the engine. He felt his way carefully on the ship's momentum and gave the order to throw the lines. The ferry was warped in and finally he heard the creaking sigh as the tire fenders rubbed the landing.

The welcoming party streamed aboard. The old lady of the river was theirs.

Wilder bent to the voice pipe. "Chief engineer!"

After a moment Tack's smiling voice came bursting into the pilothouse. "Aye, Captain!"

"Don't shut down your boiler. We'll keep steam up in case we have to run."

There was a startled pause and the smile went out of the voice. "You ask to waste fuel? It is three days until we leave the lagoon."

"Nevertheless, keep up steam."

With a ship now under his feet, Wilder was no longer sure he was content to wait for the benediction of Dr. Sing's preposterous underworld of spirits. Wilder supposed they'd be safe enough in the lagoon, even for three days. The junks would take up stations outside the channel and any stray river vendors entering the lagoon wouldn't be let out until the escape was under way. The ferry would remain a secret bottled up in the lagoon, and it wasn't likely that Amoy would be out looking for a ship that had clearly sunk. But Wilder had had enough of waiting, demons or not.

Why not pull out the moment the moon fell tomorrow night? The village needed time to transfer its belongings—but still, tomorrow night.

All Wilder had to do was overcome the wind-and-water fears of the villagers. Or take them by surprise.

Wilder worked on the ship all night. He'd moved his few things, plus the chart of the coast, into the captain's cabin below. The steersman, the captain, and a fresh bottle of whisky had been moved to the village. Wilder gathered together a party to wash down the ship and put Big Han, the lacquer carver, to work at the bows painting the ferry's new name just above the ship's eyes—*Chiku Shan*.

Cathy trailed him around the ship, taking delight in all she saw, as if she were examining a new house she might move into.

"There are an awful lot of broken windows."

"Yes."

"What's this called?"

"The hog post."

"It looks like a silly Maypole with all these wires."

Wilder sweated on the turnbuckles in an attempt to raise the sag of the hurricane deck, but the turnbuckles were all frozen with rust. He knew he ought to stop, take Cathy aside, and put her straight about her father. He would have liked to stop the chatter.

He turned and instead asked her to hunt up Mr. Tso and bring him back.

Wilder was in the engine room with Tack when Cathy's voice came gaily down the voice pipe. Mr. Tso was waiting in the pilothouse. Wilder wiped the grease off his hands and went up the ladders. He wasn't sure he was going to fool Mr. Tso, but at least he'd be logical.

Cathy had brought a pot of tea down from the village and lit the pilothouse lantern. Mr. Tso looked as if she'd got him out of bed. When Wilder glanced at the brass chronometer he was surprised to see that it was past four in the morning.

"I think it would be wise," Wilder said abruptly, "if you started moving your people aboard as soon as it gets light." He saw Cathy's eyes shift. He knew how desperately she was counting on the final three days of waiting. Jesus, he thought bitterly, he must tell her and get it over with. She had nothing left to wait for.

"There is ample time," Mr. Tso muttered softly. His wrinkled eyes gathered. What was the eminent brother trying to say?

"Of course," Wilder agreed. He knew the believing village would balk if there was any suspicion that he might try to start the escape before the favorable date.

"You have planned well, but we must now be as maneuverable as possible. There is always some risk that we may be discovered here in the lagoon. Is there any reason why the village can't live aboard for the next three days?"

"So."

"If the false smokestack in the river topples over in the tide, we ought to be in a position to leave at once."

"It would be unwise to depart on an ill-fated day."

"It might be more unwise to remain."

Wilder had long ago abandoned any impulses to change the Chinese world around him. Anyone but a fool knew he was mismatched, and it wasn't the sort of labor that appealed to Wilder. It surprised him a little that he was trying now.

"All I ask," he added, "is that we be ready in case of trouble."

Cathy forced a cup and saucer into his hands. "I think it'll be rather exciting to sit here under the noses of the Reds for three days, Captain Wilder."

Wilder put aside the tea and did his best to ignore the resentment in her voice. They saw through him, of course. Both of them. Finally Mr. Tso straightened thoughtfully.

"Perhaps there is virtue in the eminent brother's thinking. We must not take too much pride in our cleverness. I will discuss it with the other elders."

Wilder felt that he had an ally.

Cathy stood very still after the old man had gone.

"If you'll excuse me," Wilder said, "I've got work to do."

The ship was silent. Wilder found a wiper on duty in the engine room; Tack had turned in for a few hours' sleep. Wilder was impatient for the dawn. He got a lantern and made a slow inspection of the decks. The work party had made some headway against the accumulated grime and he began to take some pride in the paddle-wheeler. The hog framing and guys had long ago lost their grip on the superstructure and the crooked lines offended his seaman's eye. The saloon and texas deck doors wouldn't close and there *were* a lot of broken windows. Everything would have to be blacked out. Even if there were no paint to go round the bulkheads, the Han family would have lacquer enough for trimming the gingerbread moldings, and that would help.

He'd get it looking like something before they churned into Hong Kong.

He drifted aft on the cargo deck and gazed a long time at the spindly arms and braces and fixed buckets of the paddle wheel. It looked huge and fragile under the lantern. An old lady with a bustle, he thought tolerantly. While she was getting her new boiler the missing paddle had been replaced and she was as ready as she would ever be. She was high and narrow, he thought, and God help us in a rough sea.

But she was a ship, and he was beginning to find some affection for her.

A dry wind came in with daybreak. Wilder was washing the pilothouse windows and stopped to listen to the growing moan of the pines. The dawn sky was clear but faintly amber. He glanced at drifts of wind pulling spray off the waterfall two hundred yards away.

He returned thoughtfully to the windows.

Big Han came down early from the village. He hadn't had much sleep, but there wasn't a line on his broad, eager face.

"I apply," he said, "for third mate's job."

"Any experience?"

"None."

"Then I'll make you first mate. Is there any white lacquer in your family paint pots?"

"We use reds, yellows, blacks—no white. It's the color of death, *ch'uan-chang*."

"All right. Paint the jack staff yellow. That's the jack staff sticking up in front of the pilothouse. I want to be able to see it clearly at night, to sight by, you understand? Also, there's a name plate hanging up there. It ought to be brought up to date."

"Ah, yes. That will be a pleasure."

"We're the *Chiku Shan* now."

The name had a different flavor on Wilder's tongue. It no longer meant a walled village. It was the name of a ship, a rusty brown barn of a ship, but she floated and she had eight knots in her, and if he never did anything else he was going to get the *Chiku Shan* down Blood Alley to Hong Kong.

Nearby, the sampans loaded up with boulders and moved into the channel to finish the building-up job at the neck of the lagoon bottle. This granite graveyard, Wilder reflected, would do nicely for the Amoy patrol boat.

Wilder started a pot of tea brewing in the littered pantry and began cleaning up the place while he waited. He found odds and ends of broken crockery in the cupboards, but the best he could do was a cup without a handle. He carried the brew up the ladder to the pilothouse and relaxed at the chart table. He felt that he'd got a lot done, but now that it was light he'd want to check and oil the deck machinery. He wondered if the bow capstan could be made to work. The anchor, a heavy, old-fashioned casting with a folding stock, couldn't be raised without it. He supposed that at one time the ferry must have done duty on some swift river where she needed all that anchor weight to hold. From the verdigris on both the capstan and the anchor, he doubted that either had been used in twenty years.

The stiffening wind was music to his ears.

He turned the hot cup in his hand and studied the cracked blue pennant on its side. He found the emblem remarkable, and stared at the words. "Sacramento Steam Navigation Co." The old, bustled lady must once have churned up California waters, he realized. The cup in his hand must have been knocking about the ship for three quarters of a century.

Big Han was already at work on the jack staff with a can of yellow paint. Wilder assumed Mr. Tso had got his way with the other elders and felt the exodus from the village would start very soon. The wind went humming through the guys, there was a special dryness in the air, and Wilder thought he knew what it meant. It meant they might be able to take off that afternoon.

Anticyclone winds were coming in off the Mongolian desert. He'd met them before off the China coast. Unless he missed his guess, a dust storm was brewing. And that was just fine.

Where the hell was Mr. Tso?

During the next half hour all that showed up from the village was a work party. Wilder explained about the window blackout and had the deck cargo of vegetables shifted to the saloon, where the cooking would be done. He asked Li the carpenter to see what could be done about the doors that wouldn't close, and finally left the ship.

Once in the village, he saw that no effort was under way to pack up and leave. He found his way to the Tso courtyard, knocked, and, glancing at himself in the devil mirror fixed to the doorjamb, ran his fingers through his hair. The mirror, meant to frighten away devils, who would see their reflections and take off, reminded Wilder only that he hadn't had any sleep.

One of the women of the family ushered him into a gloomy hall and after a moment Mr. Tso came down.

Mr. Tso regretted. The elders had decided to wait before moving the village aboard. The temptation might be too great to depart before the divined time. On this point the elders distrusted their *ti-pao*.

Wilder didn't stick around. Dust was already in the air and dust could conceal them as they slipped past the ships in the outer Amoy harbor. But thanks to the doctor of magic, they weren't going anywhere.

When Wilder returned to the *Chiku Shan* for his gun, Cathy was aboard. The morning sky had turned apricot and the heated wind tugged at the sleeves of her silk blouse.

"We're staying," she said.

"I just found out."

"Tom, you don't really understand these people."

"I understand Dr. Sing. He's risking our necks with his abracadabra. I've had enough. This dust is going to get beautifully thicker. In another couple of hours you won't be able to see a hundred yards."

"We're safe here for a while. Why not—"

"This is the next best thing to a fog and we're taking it."

"What are you going to do?"

"Beat some sense in Dr. Sing's head."

"It won't work."

"Watch me."

"He'd die before he'd allow himself to lose face."

Wilder almost let her have the truth. But it would be foul and cheap to throw her father's death at her to win an argument, and he let it go and left her standing.

He picked up the Tokarev and realized that she was right. The wind-and-water man had face to preserve;

a gun might be useless. He took it anyway, left the ship, and started up the narrow stone stairway. The common Chinese saying went through his head: Money can move the gods. That might be the answer if there was money around, but that was a laugh.

By the time he reached the wall gate he was thinking more seriously of it. Old Feng, the village communist, had made a lot of money in the Philippines; where did he keep it? Wilder thought of the old pumpkin sitting in his skeleton of a Rolls-Royce—even when it rained and out of bounds to the rest of his family. Untouchable. Maybe he spent his time out there sitting on more than his hind end.

Wilder grabbed at the idea.

He saw village guards lounging in the doorways of the Feng establishment and he could hear the wailings and tempers inside. The family members had been prisoners or more than twelve hours.

At Wilder's approach a chicken fluttered off one of the headlights. The car was an old right-hand drive model, and Wilder had to break a window to get in. He found a litter of roasted watermelon-seed shells on the floor and a flowered chamber pot in one corner. He didn't quite know where to look and he felt slightly idiotic looking at all. But if money moved the gods, Old Feng's fortune might get them quickly on their way. One word from Dr. Sing and the village would stream aboard.

Wilder tried the seats, ripping upholstery and searching around. He finally dumped them into the courtyard. Villagers began to collect around him. They'd apparently never been allowed close to the old car, and seemed, from old habit, almost afraid to touch it.

Wilder found a few greasy tools under the seat and several cardboard tubes that contained cheaply colored pornographic scenes done on silk. They raised a howl from the audience. So that was how the old rice sack amused himself.

Wilder discovered a small iron box under the front seat and his hopes soared. He picked up a small, greasy wrench and thought he could twist off the brass lock. But with the wrench in his hand, he found his attention diverted. The small wrench was extraordinarily heavy. He got out his gun and with the tip scraped through the black grease along the handle. A golden scratch appeared.

Wilder stopped. There was no doubt about it. The wrench was cast out of gold. Old Feng had converted his fortune into a few greasy automobile tools and protested his poverty to his comrades. Let them search his house as they did the landlords'. He had nothing hidden like the wealthy pigs!

Wilder sent for Mr. Tso and turned the find over to him. Old Feng might be more manageable on the voyage if he knew his fortune was sailing with him. Wilder held out only the small wrench and found his way to the Sing courtyard. He had the gun and the wrench, and he'd use both if he had to. Dr. Sing was going to advance the date.

He was taken to the fortuneteller's apartment. There was no answer to their knock. A key was found, and when they entered the shabby room all they found was an abusive note to the family.

The doctor of magic had packed up his few valuables sometime before dawn and slipped away.

Chapter Fourteen

Wilder stood at the pilothouse and gazed at the exodus from the village. In the amber haze the figures moved single file down the long narrow stairway like creatures in a tapestry. They brought furniture on their backs, they came with squealing pigs under their arms, with bedding, with their family altars and pictures. They hurried. Dr. Sing's treachery had moved the village.

Mr. Tso stood now beside Wilder, dust caught in the wrinkles of his face, his anger expressing itself sadly in proverb. "*Ai*, every family cooking pot has one black spot. *An-chien-nan-fang*. The secret arrow cannot be guarded against. Now my people understand. They will go."

Wilder said nothing. Did they have an hour? He despised every moment's delay while the ship was loaded up. He called down to the engine room.

"What's your steam pressure now?"

Tack's voice was brisk and hearty in the tube. "If I believe my gauge, which is a liar, twenty-seven pounds. It is sufficient to start."

"I'm going to use full speed down the river."

"I will give it to you."

"What about fuel?"

"There is wood cut and waiting in the village."

"Better have it packed in now. I don't intend to wait around."

"Aye, Captain!"

Wilder turned to Mr. Tso. "We'll gamble on an hour. Get your people to snap it up. There isn't time to take everything."

"They labor quickly. They understand that they have been made fools of and anger drives them."

"You questioned the night watchman?"

The old man sighed wearily. "There is no doubt what our *Fêng-Shui* doctor plans for us. The watchman saw him before five, strange and nervous under the lantern. He expressed a desire to walk for the last time among the pines. *Ai-tsai!* He will not be back, except to accuse us and denounce his family as traitors!"

Wilder took no pleasure in recalling his first uneasy impression of the fortuneteller. No one had suspected a Red spot on the Sing family cooking pot, and Wilder had been no wiser than the rest of them. He had put the doctor of magic down as a mystic crank, vain and ambitious and troublesome, but not a Communist. Well, the little bastard had been cunning. He had waited until the ferry was in the lagoon and now he must be somewhere on the road that cut through the hills behind Chiku Shan and ended across the water from Amoy. What a plum he would deliver into the hands of the commissars! One hundred and eighty enemies of the People on one of the People's own ships! Sure, and that would make the little guy a first-class People's hero. Hadn't he tricked the traitors into waiting like crackbrains while he ran for help? Perhaps the hawks and dogs in Peiping would even hold a banquet for the heroic *Fêng-Shui* doctor!

"His family loses face," Mr. Tso muttered bitterly. "It is better to spawn a black turtle than such a son."

Wilder was glad when the old man left. He was sorry for the family of dollmakers, but he had other matters to think about. He glanced at the Japanese barometer, its glass face cracked, and the clock. Dr. Sing had been gone four hours—on foot. Had a truck picked him up on the road? He might instead have cut over to the river and flagged a sampan. Once he reached the Amoy commissars, it was going to take a lot of arm waving to convince them of his preposterous story. But eventually they'd believe him. The renegade was, after all, of the village itself, and they had only to send the patrol boat to investigate the crowned funnel poking out of the muddy waters in the estuary.

Then the patrol boat would surely come steaming up the river to Chiku Shan. Well, they'd planned to lure it into the lagoon, but now the timetable was stepped up. Was there an hour?

Wilder left the pilothouse. He saw a grandmother stubbornly nailing a devil mirror over one of the cabin doorways. On the cargo deck he warned Big Han to keep the villagers from piling all their stuff along the bow. The growing weight forward was already lifting the paddle wheel out of the water.

"I do my best, *ch'uan-chang*."

Outraged chickens, dust, and human confusion swirled about them and Wilder wondered if they'd ever be ready. He moved aft and saw Li the carpenter attempting to build pens for the pigs and ducks and goats. The deck was jammed with bundles of clothes, dishes, pots and pans, gilt-framed pictures of dour grandfathers. Pet birds jumped about in fragile cages and ducks waddled about imperiously, poking into things. When Wilder saw the first of the coffins being carried aboard he all but blew up. Christ, he thought, even the dead are going!

"*K'uai-k'uai!*" Wilder shouted. "Quickly."

The decks were gritty under his sandals. He stared at the endless ant stream from the high wall gate—baskets of rice, clay household idols, carved screens, flowerpots, beds. Where did they think they would put it all?

The haze was thickening; the pines that rose around the lagoon had become a crown of burned shadows. Wilder noticed another painted coffin on its way down the stairway, like a funeral procession.

He turned away angrily and wondered why he wasn't seeing Cathy around.

At a quarter to ten the decks were almost impassable, but still they came. Aft of the paddle wheel the sampans, loaded high with boulders, sat in the water almost to their gunwales. Mr. Tso had devised a trap that would lock the patrol boat in the lagoon and prevent armed interference as the ferry sailed out of Amoy waters. It had long been planned and Dr. Sing would make it easier. The sampans waited.

Wilder wanted to pull out in fifteen minutes.

Little wood came down from the village and Wilder thought Tack must have had trouble pulling cousins away from their family treasures to pack fuel. The little ferry couldn't possibly hold enough wood to take her all the way to Hong Kong.

Wilder decided to worry about that later.

He watched for a glint of blonde hair; as far as he could tell, Cathy hadn't been aboard in hours. He saw that the Feng family was on its way down from the village now—at gunpoint. He stopped to watch Old Feng bellowing through the haze, his arms jerking in protest. The entire family was held together by ropes around their waists; they moved down the steps like a blue cotton caterpillar.

"Have you seen Miss Grainger around?"

Big Han looked up from the ancient tripod machine gun he was setting between the bows. The gun looked like something that had seen duty in the days of Sun Yat-sen.

"No, *ch'uan-chang.*"

Wilder left the ship as the Fengs reached the lagoon landing. He got a good look at the old man for the first time. Anger was parboiling his round, silken face.

Bandits! Kidnappers! His stout hips shook as he flailed his arms, and then he saw Wilder's American face. His sweat-stained straw hat seemed willing to fly off his head. Where had the running dog come from? What is this madness that overtakes our village cousins? Pig! Capitalist dog!

Wilder pushed past them and fought his way up the stone steps. Finally furnace wood was coming down. Once inside the walls of the village, Wilder was struck by the air of final desolation. He saw torches moving through the haze. The village was setting fire to what it couldn't take along.

He passed a sobbing woman on the run, crying out the name of a child. He caught her shoulders.

"What is it?"

"My smallest one. I cannot find him."

She had hardly cried out the words when a boy in his best cottons, his arms loaded with joss sticks, came grinning through the haze. The woman broke out of Wilder's hands, and he hurried down to the Grainger house.

He found Susu smoking a cigarette with preposterous calmness.

"Get down to the ferry."

"We no go."

"Grab what you can and clear out! Where's Cathy?"

"My no savvy. She go somewhere. We no wanchee makee trip."

Wilder exploded. He let her know Dr. Grainger was dead and ordered her to pack what she could in the remaining minutes. Tears sprang into her great eyes, and he didn't hang around for the rest of it.

Fires were already leaping out of the village windows. Wilder cut across to the high wall, found a flight of steps, and ran past the stone crenelations. He passed battlements and towers and a moment later heard a dog barking. Koxinga.

He found Cathy sitting in the tower broken by the gnarled pine tree. She was gazing vacantly at the dust and wind-swept rooftops below. She didn't turn.

"Hello, Torn."

He pulled her around and slapped her hard. It startled her and a vicious stare leaped into her eyes and he welcomed it. Rage might take some of the curse off what he had to say.

"Your dad's been killed, Cathy. There's nothing left for you here."

Her nostrils began to flare. "You're lying."

"I've known it for a couple of days. I just didn't have the guts to tell you, and I'm sorry."

"I'm not going on the boat. They *wouldn't* kill him! They need him!"

"I'm not lying, baby. His patient died and they decided to turn it into some high-grade hate propaganda. They dragged him to a People's court and everybody in Swatow got in the act. He's dead."

The gritty wind stung their faces. Her self-possession faltered; she turned and stared once more at the fires springing up below. Wilder moved a step forward and took her lightly in his hands.

"I'm sorry, baby."

"Had he been drinking?"

Wilder hesitated. "No."

She turned in his arms and held her hair in the wind. "You're lying." A great coolness came into her eyes and he saw there wasn't going to be any emotion. He'd taken hold of a kid and somehow, during those few seconds, she'd changed into a woman.

"There's no point in standing here, is there?" she muttered.

"None at all."

"There's not much I care to take."

Chapter Fifteen

"Stand by!"

The engine room answered Wilder's bell. The sun burned a fierce ring through the yellow gloom and the funnel smoke blackened the dust. Big Han had enlarged the eyes at the ferry's bows, painting them a fierce red and giving their tadpole shapes an angry tilt; Fukien eyes that would guide them through the Strait to Hong Kong. The brass clock over Wilder's head said ten-twenty.

He bent out the window with the megaphone. "Cast off down there!"

Big Han relayed the order and Wilder watched long enough to make sure the lines were cleared. Behind the village walls, spires of smoke spread into the haze.

The steamboat was poled away from the stone landing and Wilder returned to the voice tube.

"Slow speed ahead."

"Aye, Captain."

"Be ready to slam on the brakes if I can't make the turn."

The slow beat of the piston came through the ship and the paddle wheel began to rumble in the water. Wilder wiped the sweat off his hands and took the helm gently. The jack staff drifted off the waterfall ahead and passed along the wall of the lagoon. Wilder kept turning the wheel to bring the ship about in the granite bottle.

The waiting was over.

A wailing broke out along the decks under him; the moment of abandoning their birthplace struck like a knife. Wilder tried to shut it out of his ears. The ferry was lazy in the turn and the far bank approached much too quickly.

He pulled the bell cord to stop and reverse. He had shut the wheelhouse doors to keep out the curious and his shirt clung to his back. The junks and the sampans were outside the lagoon ready to give a warning signal if the patrol boat came growling up the river. He backed the ship gingerly until the stern was almost under the waterfall, and then began twisting the wheel again to the left. He rang for slow speed ahead and finally the high-banked channel stood in front of the bows.

In another moment they'd be out of the neck of the bottle.

The ferry took a list to port as the villagers rushed across the ship to gaze for a last time at their burning past. A swooping wind rattled the pilothouse windows and the wide river opened up before them.

He saw Cathy standing at the bow.

The sampans were there, their stones now covered over with branches. He could vaguely make out the shape of the first junk far to port, waiting to light a string of firecrackers if the patrol boat appeared. The other junk stood somewhere ahead of it, downriver, obscured by the haze.

Wilder turned the paddle-wheeler upriver, away from Amoy, and his optimism mounted.

He steamed through the dust for better than half a mile and made a wide turn in the river, pointing the bows toward Amoy, where they belonged.

They had to wait for the patrol boat. If they met it on the river it would blow them to bits.

The final delay.

Wilder watched Cathy below, and by reversing the paddle wheel against the tide he attempted to keep the *Chiku Shan* in position. By the time Cathy had come aboard, all the texas cabins had been taken, and he'd put her in his own. Between the three of them and despite Susu's streaming eyes, they'd got some clothes and medicines out of the house, and, foolishly, a hoarded bottle of imported curry powder. Wilder had set fire to the house and Cathy's celestial bed.

Occasional junks and sampans, coolies staring, drifted past them, and Wilder could imagine the confusion in their minds. Word must already have spread along the river that the ferryboat had burned and sunk, and yet there it stood like a red-eyed monster, the voices of children and ducks and pigs shooting out from its decks.

But the patrol boat, if it ever came, wouldn't see them at this distance through the haze. Now it *had* to come.

When half an hour had passed, Wilder's patience began to desert him. What if the commissars had refused to believe Dr. Sing's tale? It would be suicide for the paddle-wheeler to proceed downriver until the patrol boat was immobilized.

He could hear Big Han's voice on the deck trying to get his cousins to clear away their belongings.

"*Tsou-k'uai!* You think we want to look like a junkyard when we reach Hong Kong?"

At eleven-forty a string of firecrackers began to pop in the distance.

The patrol boat had shown up in the river.

Wilder yanked the bell cord.

Full speed ahead!

The paddle wheel began its forward chunking and the decks began to vibrate. They were at last taking off for good.

Speed built up under them and Wilder had to imagine what was happening forward of them in the haze. If the patrol boat expected to find the ferry tied up in the lagoon, it must already be steaming into the channel. The sampans would move in after it, sinking themselves at the entrance. The bottom there had been raised, boulder by boulder; the patrol boat would barely skim over the stones. It would never skim out. The sampans, with their final cargoes of rock, would bring the channel bottom almost to the surface of the water.

The bow waves began to curl and spread, and the wind hummed in the guys. Wilder's hands tightened on the wheel as they drew closer to the channel. He saw now that the machine gun at the bow was manned and that another had been set up.

The moments stiffened. A black pall marked the village bluff through the dust, and then they could make out familiar details. The patrol boat was nowhere in sight.

Wilder reached for the whistle and let it scream. One of the village junks came into view and Wilder saw one of the sampan coolies, wet from his swim from the channel, being pulled aboard. There was a great waving and pointing of arms.

The patrol boat was in the lagoon.

Fine, Wilder thought. Splendid.

He kept the whistle screaming as the channel passed on their port side. They'd recognized the familiar sound in the lagoon and had come storming out.

Branches and leaves floated in the neck of the bottle where the sampans had sunk themselves.

And then the gray wooden nose of the patrol boat popped into sight, a soldier straddling it, a Bren gun in his hands. An enraged whistle came blasting from the channel—and then the trap was sprung.

The patrol boat hit the stone wall that hadn't been there moment before.

Wood exploded and Wilder saw the soldier pitched into the air like a green beetle. The boat seemed to split open like a ripe melon and its racing screw sent it grating across the submerged rocks. A tumultuous shouting broke from the *Chiku Shan's* decks.

Wilder held onto the whistle a moment longer. It seemed a moment for celebration. The concussion, he thought, must have knocked the seagoing comrades through their bulkheads.

They stopped to pick up the sampan coolies and junkmen and put the Chinese captain and steersman off the ferry. Wilder got Tack on the voice tube.

"If you want a last look at home, take it now."

"Thank you, no, Captain."

"Then give us full speed ahead."

"Aye, Captain!"

Chapter Sixteen

They hit a chop at the mouth of the river and the ferry began to pitch, slapping its flat bottom against the water. An empty wine bottle lost its balance in a corner and began to roll across the pilothouse linoleum.

Except for the thrashing of the paddle wheel, there seemed no sound in the dust-blown estuary.

Wilder followed the hand signals that came slow and sure beside him. His fisherman-pilot stood barefooted at one of the windows, guiding him now through the islands of the estuary. They would follow the south shore out into the Strait of Formosa and then Wilder would be on his own.

The bottle rolled between Wilder's feet and he kicked it aside.

If the dust held, they would steam well out of sight of Amoy and Kulangsu, a mile beyond and just north of the estuary. They ought to slip by easily in about an hour. It would seem strange, Wilder thought, to pass without seeing the familiar landmarks—the preposterous granite boulder called Wellington's Nose, the flags of the signal station, the green buoy marking the wreck just off Cornwallis Stone. They were landmarks out of the past and he supposed he'd never take bearings on them again.

Junks began to take shape in the rusty gloom; the ferry was crossing the traffic lane. They cut past a Hakka boat from the interior with its lofty flared bow and triangular sails. It vanished in the haze and a string of cargo sampans came up and Wilder considered cutting speed.

But he didn't.

To Wilder it seemed forever before the fisherman spread his hands with satisfaction and turned to him with a fine grin.

"The shore is there—maybe hundred-forty *chang* distance."

"Thank you."

Wilder spun the helm and the jack staff began to come across the dirty, wrinkled water. He couldn't see land, but he was willing to take his pilot's word for it. They nosed into their own smoke, carried forward by the wind, and the bows slit the incoming tide.

Even with the wind behind them, Wilder could feel the drag of the current, and he knew they were losing speed. He bent to the voice tube.

"Chief engineer!"

"Aye, Captain."

"Let's not wallow in the estuary all afternoon. Can you give us more power?"

"It is possible, but you burn us out of wood before we reach the Strait."

"What pressure are you carrying?"

"Thirty-four pounds. I blow up the old boiler with

thirty-six, but the new one is steel. Maybe she hold forty pounds."

Wilder's experience had been with high-pressure engines and the readings Tack gave him had an incredible ring over the voice tube. Forty pounds! Could that kind of pressure ever get them to Hong Kong?

"All right, never mind," Wilder said after a moment. "Let's not blow ourselves out of the estuary."

Wilder sat on his anxiety to get into familiar waters. He had some recollection of a fort at Taipan Point, marking the southern tip of the estuary, and once past it he'd know exactly where he was. There'd be seven long miles of the outer harbor to slip past, but the haze was one of God's footsteps.

Sampans scattered from the noisy chunking of their wheel. It no longer mattered what the river coolies thought. Let them gape. A Hangchow junk with sea-washed phoenix eyes veered across the *Chiku Shan's* bow, but Wilder held the wheel steady and the junk scraped past.

At one o'clock they came within the dark shadow of Taipan Point and Wilder's pilot deserted him. He knew nothing of the waters outside of the estuary.

Wilder thanked him and wished him a pleasant voyage. He was almost glad to have the pilothouse to himself. Mr. Tso had got him a ship and got him out of the river. The rest was going to be Wilder's show, one way or the other. A moment later a soft knock came at the door. "Who the hell is it?"

"I thought perhaps you'd like me to fetch you something to eat." It was Cathy.

"I'm not hungry."

"All right."

"Look—don't go." He hadn't meant to bite her head off. "Come in if you want to."

She had a kerchief around her hair. Her face was pale and her lips looked as though they might smile, but they didn't.

"There's a bench against the bulkhead," Wilder said. "Make yourself inconspicuous for a few moments."

"I won't say a word. But if you get hungry, just whistle."

Within the next few minutes he managed to forget that she was in the deckhouse with him. He dropped speed to cut the funnel glow and moved out from shore and the point. The outer harbor lay somewhere in the dust dead ahead.

He'd bounce around the fort and risk a mile or so of the inner harbor. He felt certain they must be in advance of any alert, but he didn't want to move within sight of the fort. Any visiting ships at anchor in the outer channel probably didn't know the ferryboat existed.

They had steamed less than five minutes when Wilder saw one of the machine gunners pop to his feet and freeze.

An instant later Wilder picked up the outline across the bow. He spun the wheel and the ferry began to rumble in a sharp turn. Two ships materialized in the brown fog dead ahead. Before the wake had swung around they had drifted close enough to make out more than vague shapes at anchor. They weren't freighters.

"Gunboats," Wilder snapped. "Two of them. Half the goddamn Red navy is sitting out there!"

He held the wheel hard over until they all but doubled over their wake, and the gunboats faded. From his brief glimpse of a single stack and five-inch gun turrets forward and aft, he took them for destroyer escorts.

Cathy was on her feet. "They must have seen us."

"Yes."

Wilder found fresh sweat on his brows. They had certainly been spotted, but they weren't in trouble yet unless the alert was out. The next moments would tell.

They slipped past the fort, shrouded in haze, and the clock over Wilder's head ticked off the minutes.

An hour later they were still alone, bucketing past the lower end of the inner harbor and out into the Strait of Formosa. Wilder cut speed to save wood and to play safe. He liked the cover of dust and didn't want to risk outrunning it before night. It was all he had to work with if the DE's were finally awakened and came steaming after them with twenty knots in their bellies. And if their radar sets hadn't broken down, even the dust wouldn't be enough.

Some two hours later, off the sand peaks of House Hill Point, they thrashed out of the haze into startling sunlight.

Chapter Seventeen

The *Chiku Shan* came bucketing through the dust curtain like some astonished night animal. Wilder squinted. The bows looked grimy and senile under the blue sweep of sky. Crisp sunlight glinted off the pilothouse windows and Cathy stood peering at the sudden, razor-sharp horizon.

"Must we go back?"

"That's right." He started the wheel over and it creaked mournfully. With the gunboats sitting perhaps fifteen miles behind them off Taipan Point, there was no question in his mind.

"It's beautiful out there, isn't it?"

"It's deadly out there. We'll sit in the dust until

nightfall."

He saw the faint drop of her shoulders. It hurt to go back, and with the wheel spinning in his hands he realized for the first time that he was tired. A moment before there hadn't been a muscle in his body. Now he felt them all, and he despised the oak grips in his hands. The paddle-wheeler had slipped out of the estuary, past Taipan Point and the outer harbor, and now, they were splitting their own wake.

The dusty gloom once more darkened the windows. They roved some three miles back along the coast, bobbing over an occasional swell, and Wilder edged to port to get well out of the sea lane. There was foul ground along shore, he knew. He dropped one of the windows and ordered a couple of villagers to the bow with bamboo poles. They poked the depths and the *Chiku Shan* moved slowly, like a blind man with a cane.

Cathy turned from the window and her eyes accused him of timidity. "I wouldn't be surprised if those gunboats refused to take orders from Amoy."

"Fine."

"We might have kept going."

"We might have."

"But we didn't."

"Let's not get ourselves in more of a jam than becomes us, baby. Once they cut their red tape, if that's what's kept them off our tail so far, their twenty knots will make our eight look pretty silly. Maybe they're already out in the murk looking for us. Maybe anything. My throat's dry and suddenly I'm hungry. What do you want me to whistle?"

A black rock came up to port and Wilder swung around it. This seemed as good a stopping place as any, and he rang off speed. The steam cocks whistled.

"Cousins!" he shouted, bending out the window. "Get

the anchor over the side!"

He waited until the outsized hook went plummeting into the water, rattling a heavy rust-scaled chain after it. They'd save fuel and maybe he could flake out for an hour or so. There'd be an unrelieved night watch ahead of him. He supposed it was going to be a sweet chore getting all that metal aboard again with the capstan frozen, but he didn't feel like jockeying the ship around until dark.

He caught Big Han's eye. "See if there's a hacksaw in the engine room. Post someone at the chain. If we have to pull out in a hurry, we'll cut ourselves loose."

"Yes, *ch'uan-chang!*"

Big Han made a brisk, compliant gesture and Wilder left the window. He saw that Cathy had left the pilothouse and an uneasy cynicism settled over him. Did she take him for a coward? Let her think what she liked. But he had a growing sense of her own diminishing enthusiasm for the voyage, and that bothered him more.

Wilder met Mr. Tso along the texas deck and saw that devil mirrors had been put up outside all the cabin doors. The old man greeted him with wrinkles and warm eyes.

"We are delayed long?"

"Not long."

"Our seasick would like to stop forever."

"What's been done with the Fengs?"

"Most lie sick in the big room. Their grandfather we keep guarded—there—in the cabin. We have warned the family he will be killed if they try to make trouble for us, and it will be so. There will be no trouble, eminent brother."

"I'll try to keep them seasick. It shouldn't be hard."

"Frankly—" The old man paused. "I think most of the family is pleased, now that they understand what we do."

"There's still too much stuff blocking the passageways. It ought to be squared away."

"We are making progress."

When Wilder entered the saloon it seemed to him that half the village lay rolled up on deck in patched *pukais*, waiting to die of seasickness. A wood stove had been set up at one end, and the fumes of community cooking, mixed with the smoke of the unvented stove, lay over the saloon like a disagreeable fog. Only the kids seemed unaware, scrambling around between the prone shapes of their parents, while birds sang in their cages hung around the wooden stanchions.

Wilder stopped one of the villagers carrying in wood and told him to get the stove vented before they started a fire in the saloon.

"And get all the doors open. These poor devils need fresh air."

Below, on the boiler deck, he saw that the animals were faring better. The goats were securely tethered and the hogs penned just forward of the paddle wheel. The fowl crawled over each other in rattan cages. A villager was slaughtering a pig and the hide lay spread on deck like a giant soiled bat. There'd be pork for dinner for those with stomach enough to eat it.

Wilder moved back up the ladder toward the captain's stateroom, smelled heavy incense through the dust, and discovered that one of the cabins had been set aside for the altar, the ancestor sticks, the painted idols.

When he entered his cabin he saw that Cathy's scorn had passed as quickly as it had come. Her smile entirely ignored the moments in the pilothouse, as if she had acted foolishly and preferred to forget it. She had taken down the soiled green curtain from the pantry doorway, stripped the bunk, and remade it with her own linen.

"The place has possibilities," she remarked thoughtfully. "Do you mind if I change things around?"

"Suit yourself. Where's your dog?"

"He's taken to the bathtub. Never seen one before—a real one, I mean. Look, I managed to stock the pantry with some fresh eggs and rice and things. What would you like?"

"A small T-bone steak would be fine."

He got Koxinga out of the bathtub, a claw-footed affair that went with the gingerbread woodwork, and felt better when he had shaved and cleaned up. He could hear Cathy fussing around with dishes in the pantry. It was going to be awkward, both of them in the same stateroom, and he supposed he'd better see what he could do about finding sleeping quarters for himself.

Cathy had set the table from the graveyard of pantry dishes and met him with eggs sizzling in a frying pan.

"Did you think I couldn't cook?" she muttered.

"It never occurred to me to wonder."

They ate together and the ferry creaked gently at its anchor chain. Wilder kept glancing at the portholes for any signs of a thinning haze, but it was holding. They ought to be able to get under way safely at about seven o'clock. He tried to forget the pair of DE's. They had looked U.S.-built, probably a gift to the Nationalists before the Reds had got them. If they had maintained their radar equipment, the escape was going to be a washout.

"Tom?"

"I like my steaks this way. Medium rare."

"We'll be going past Swatow, won't we?"

He looked up. Her green eyes were entirely sincere and hopeful. It was one of the few times when he could read her mind, and he didn't like what he saw. "Cathy, he's dead."

"I want to be put ashore there. I saw a lifeboat. It would only delay you a few minutes."

"Cut it out."

"I've got to make sure, Tom. Don't you understand? He may need help. They *wouldn't* kill him. They're desperate for doctors. Perhaps they put him in jail, but they wouldn't kill him. I'm sure of it."

He felt a sort of off-beat anger rising to his lips, but he held his tongue. Swatow lay some hundred miles south and Wilder expected to make the area sometime during the second night of travel, but he had no intention of stopping. Why didn't she stop kidding herself? Her old man drank and got himself in trouble and maybe she was used to getting him out of it. But this time it had been for keeps. "The papers carried the story, Cathy."

"The papers are almost always wrong."

"For God's sake," he said. "Break into tears. Beat your fists against the bulkhead. Get it out of your system. They've killed him, Cathy, and he doesn't need you anymore. You're grabbing at straws."

"I've got to make sure. I can't go to Hong Kong, Tom, not if there's a chance."

"There isn't. No one's getting off."

"Is that final?"

His voice softened. "I'm sorry, baby. It's final."

"All right. That's all I wanted to know."

Later she cleared off the dishes and he stretched out in his clothes on the bunk and went to sleep.

Chapter Eighteen

Big Han awoke him roughly.

"Quickly, *ch'uan-chang!* A ship approaches! Quickly! Wake up!"

Wilder stumbled out on deck to see for himself. The sun was setting and the air stood inflamed.

"See—there, there, *ch'uan-chang!*"

Wilder saw it. The wind had shifted, blowing to the southwest, and carried with it the black funnel smoke of an approaching ship.

"All right," Wilder snapped. "Cut the anchor chain and goddamned fast."

He hurried up the ladder to the wheelhouse and tried to bring himself awake. Gunboat? Deep water must be less than a quarter of a mile off. Freighter? What the hell was it making smoke out there?

"Engine room! Stand by!"

They were a sitting duck for radar and five-inch guns, and now he cursed the anchor and would be glad to see the last of it. He dropped one of the pilothouse windows and studied the smoke drifting over them. The ship must be close; the smoke was only beginning to break up and spread. He glanced at the villager at the anchor chain. The hacksaw shrieked. Wilder hurried to the bow.

"Get some rags and muffle the sounds! That ship out there may be blind, but it's not deaf!"

"The saw is dull."

"*K'uai-k'uai!* Quickly!"

Wilder climbed back into the pilothouse, watching the smoke as he went. It was moving fast. The ship out there had speed. She was no freighter.

The gunboat. Amoy had certainly got word that its

Patrol boat had been abruptly decommissioned in the lagoon, plus a dozen reports of the ferry's movements through the estuary. The DE's had been put to work.

Now he sweated out the possibility of radar. What the Chinese didn't know about electronics their Russian big brothers did, and he expected to hear the whine of the first shell at any instant.

He heard the distant crack of a bow wave.

Well, what were the bastards waiting for? The stern-wheeler must be damned near life size on the radar screen.

The muted rasp of the hacksaw below measured out the seconds. The telltale smoke moved steadily forward, well ahead of them now, but clearly visible as a stain across the haze.

Suddenly Wilder leaned out the window and made a gesture to knock off the saw.

The gunboat was passing them by.

Wilder held his breath until the last signs of smoke had passed. The villagers waited at the bow, like figures in a tableau, for some new order from the pilothouse.

Wilder bent to the engine-room voice tube. "You can relax down there. We'll stick around a couple of hours."

"Could you see it?"

"No, but it went by like the Red navy. They're onto us."

"Even the Red navy has radar, Captain."

"Then they took us for just another offshore rock on their scope. Maybe we've blundered into the answer to their radar. They're looking for a moving pip and we're as solid as this rock beside us."

Wilder wiped the sweat off his face and considered lighting an incense cone to all the ineptly trained radarmen in the Red navy.

It was eight-thirty before Wilder considered it safe

to finish off the anchor chain and get out. By its gift of speed the DE must have drawn well ahead and left them out of radar range.

The ship went chunking through a flat night sea, dirtying the stars with chimney smoke. At two o'clock Wilder estimated his position as somewhere off Black Head, and if he could trust his chart, a nightmare of rocks would stand ahead of them in about an hour. There was Rees Pass, four hundred yards wide if he could find it, and some dangerous tidal eddies if he didn't. He decided instead to cut out for deeper water and try to swing around the whole mess. He could only guess at the gunboat's position. He had charted its probable course south to the greatest distance the ferry might have covered in the time since she had left Amoy, and it wasn't far. Finding nothing in his scope, the Red captain would come about, Wilder thought, and steam northeast with an eye on Formosa—possibly to join the other DE in searching those more logical waters. The sea lane between Amoy and Formosa would appear to be the best hunting ground, despite anything Dr. Sing might have said. One long night of steaming would have got the paddle-wheeler directly across the Strait, and the commissars would mark that the pressing area to search. Hadn't Mr. Tso pointed that out? There would be time enough to send the gunboats south if the night netted them nothing. Hong Kong was comfortably far off, and the ferryboat had the speed of a turtle.

Shortly before three-thirty the paddle wheel stopped.

The sudden silence brought a chill to Wilder's spine. He got on the voice tube.

"What's wrong down there?"

"The steam line is clogging, Captain. We fix. It is nothing."

"How long will it take?"

"I will do the job myself."

"Chief engineer."

"Aye, Captain."

"The next goddamned time you decide to stop the ship, let me know. I'm funny that way."

Wilder left the tube swearing. Did Tack think he was master of the ship? Wilder let the wheel swing free and cupped a flashlight over his chart. He had pulled out into deep water, and if the steam line delayed them more than an hour there was a question whether he could make the coast and an anchorage of some sort before daylight. The Rees Islands must be to starboard of them, he thought, but he disliked the thought of coming anywhere near them.

He moved down the chart to the Brothers Islets, which he thought lay some fourteen miles off the coast. If he couldn't make shore, he'd try for the Brothers, he decided. Anything would be better than being caught at sea when dawn broke. He felt, without knowing for sure, that the Brothers would be uninhabited. He remembered them as craggy, inhospitable places, but they might offer a protected cove to hide in.

At four-thirty there was still no word from the engine room and Wilder could raise no one on the voice pipe. The ship creaked gently in the tide and the silence got on Wilder's nerves. He was conscious again of his fatigue. He'd had an hour's sleep since they'd grabbed the ferry and it seemed now a week ago.

Shortly before five o'clock they were under way again. Wilder stared at the compass, wondering if he were crazy to trust it, and set a course for the Brothers. If the two islets were where he had marked them on his chart, the stern-wheeler ought to be tied up by dawn. Fine. He'd sleep all day.

Big Han entered the pilothouse with a steaming pot of tea.

"My wife sends this up to you, *ch'uan-chang*. She is afraid everyone forgets you up here alone. She is a worrier, my wife, but a good woman."

The pot filled the wheelhouse with its fragrance and Wilder was glad for Big Han's worrier of a wife. "We're looking for two small islands a couple of miles apart," he said. "Wake up one of your sharp-eyed cousins and put him on the roof of the pilothouse. We've got to find them in the dark."

"I will go myself."

"Leave me a cup and take the teapot with you."

A moment later Wilder heard Big Han clattering overhead. The sea was being good to them and they slid under the stars with preposterous assurance. It had been a day for thumbing their noses at the Reds; every mile they covered was a victory. The escape seemed almost easy.

The cup grew cold in Wilder's hand. At a quarter to six there was still no signal from the roof that any islets had bulked up against the stars. A salt breeze swept through the open pilothouse windows, and if it did nothing else, it kept Wilder awake. The skin of his face felt as stiff as leather; his calves ached and his spine had turned to glass. Where were those two goddamned islets?

"Awake up there, cousin?" he shouted.

"I see nothing, *ch'uan-chang*."

Wilder's jaws began to tighten. The sun was going to catch them paddling in the middle of nowhere and this time there was no curtain of dust to wrap themselves in. Had he been accurate in charting the Brothers opposite Jokako Bay? He glanced again at the compass leering up from its binnacle. How old was it? Had it ever been checked and corrected?

A cock began to crow from the boiler deck.

The crowing, eager and raucous, spread over the softening darkness like something manic and bewitched. Wilder swore.

He scanned the horizon and a moment later it was there, the first yellow stain of dawn.

It jarred him.

It lay some fifty degrees off the port bow.

He looked again at the lying compass needle. This grandfather of all compasses must be thirty degrees off! He spun the wheel to starboard and glowered. His southeasterly bearing could only have been taking them toward the shoals and overfalls of Formosa Banks. He wanted to yank the compass out by its binnacle.

The sun rose impatiently, almost like a cork out of water, but before Wilder felt the dawn light spread across his skin he had spotted the jagged crown of an island to the southwest. Big Han yelled out and Wilder thanked him.

He got the Brothers on either side of his jack staff. They had been passing several miles to seaward. The horizon was stiff and deserted. They seemed to have Blood Alley entirely to themselves.

Wilder began to distrust their incredible luck.

Chapter Nineteen

They crept in the cool shadow of the larger Brother.

A sheer cliff hovered over them and flocks of black cormorants, gulls, and fish hawks scattered from their rocky perches at the noisy chunking of the paddle wheel. The smaller Brother, rigid in the water and square-topped, stood across a two-mile channel to starboard.

It was past seven o'clock.

Wilder circled the islet, swinging far around a reef hooked to its southern tip, and was satisfied that they were alone except for the birds. He chose his spot. The reef would give some protection from the current; the crumbling bluff would hide them from any sea traffic passing through the channel.

It would have to do.

Wilder nosed the ferry gingerly toward the shallows and the bird-clad rocks. Villagers went over the side with lines and waded ashore, warping the *Chiku Shan* in from the outcroppings. Wings slapped and the air seesawed with a thousand resentful voices. Shadows fluttered across the decks and the water sparkled as if sequins were being washed ashore.

Wilder took his stiff hands off the wheel and smiled capriciously. He'd brought the flat-bottomed scow some sixty miles out of Amoy and the fact began to astonish him. Maybe they were going to make it. They sat rubbing their shoulders against an islet in the Strait of Formosa, and no one knew it but the birds.

It was past ten before Wilder could think of getting some sleep. The starboard side of the ferry lay exposed to any ship passing eastward of the Brothers, and Wilder organized a working party to collect bushes on the island for camouflage. Tack explained that they had been burning over a cord of wood an hour and the bins were half empty, but the island was treeless. The next night Wilder would have to find a wooded anchorage.

The birds went caterwauling around the ship in a tireless merry-go-round.

The bushes came in and were spread along the starboard side and tied to the funnel and hog post. Some of the Fengs volunteered and were put to work. Finally a beady-eyed pelican, braver than the others, took up a position on the funnel crown and watched aloofly. Wilder began to see toddlers on deck with large sections of fat bamboo lashed to their backs—life preservers against a tumble overboard.

"We are concealed," Big Han said, grinning at their mat of bushes. "Now we sleep, yes?"

"I think you'd better get some lookouts up on the island. I want to be awakened any time a ship comes in sight."

"As you wish, *ch'uan-chang*."

"And look—better not put any of the Fengs as lookouts."

"I understand."

Even with the old man as hostage, Wilder thought, one of his dedicated cousins or nephews might decide to attempt a signal. He supposed it would absorb too much village man power to lock up and guard the whole family; he would go along with Mr. Tso's device up to the point of trusting any of the Fengs.

On the texas deck he could hear the Red elder groaning like a walrus in his cabin. Seasick. Splendid. He passed the two guards at the door and stopped for a moment.

"They ought to be able to hear that all the way to the mainland."

"To us it is a happy sound."

"If he gets better, let me know. I'll try to find some rough water."

When he reached the captain's quarters he could hear Cathy in the bathtub. He supposed he'd better grab a blanket and bed down in the pilothouse. He was glad he didn't have to face her now. She'd come up with this magnificent nonsense of abandoning the voyage at Swatow and he doubted that a night's sleep had brought her to her senses. He didn't feel like squaring off again. He took up the folded blanket from the foot of the bunk and Koxinga growled behind the bathroom door.

"Tom, is that you?"

Her voice was unexpectedly bright and warm.

"I was just leaving," he said.

"Wait. I'll be right out and fix you something to eat."

He stood for an uncertain moment in the center of the cabin. He didn't feel hungry. He heard the bath water begin to tinkle down the drain and, glancing at the badly set door, he thought of Cathy behind it, standing ankle-deep in the old-fashioned tub, water slipping off her shoulders and thighs and breasts. The thought amused him.

"Tom, are you still there?"

"I'm still here."

"Look, I found an old sack of something hidden in the pantry. I think it's coffee. Why don't you boil it and see what happens?"

He found the old sack. It looked and smelled completely stale, but it was coffee. He turned up the dented parts of a percolator and got it organized. Even as the thought of Cathy and Swatow harassed him, he was forced to admire her reckless determination. Admit it, he thought, smiling. There's something to this kid. She'll take on all of Red China and never mind the odds. Odds? What odds? Well, at least she knew herself—she knew Hong Kong would be pure torture if there was the slightest chance that Dr. Grainger had been left behind alive.

He got a fire going under the pot and wondered if he'd have to tie her down when they reached the Swatow area the next morning. Had she thought of pushing off in the small lifeboat? It was hardly more than a dinghy and she could handle it. He stopped and thought how strange and empty it would be to finish the trip without Cathy aboard. Maybe he'd better break up the lifeboat and send it to the furnace for firewood.

He left the pantry as Cathy came out of the bathroom. It was a moment Wilder knew instantly he could never forget. She appeared before him in a flowing nimbus of pale silk, her blonde hair quickly but smartly brushed. The kimono sash was tight against the smooth field of her stomach and he felt as if he'd never really seen her before. She looked extravagantly feminine and lovely and he knew he must be staring at her with the air of a blind man suddenly given the gift of sight. My God, he thought, where have I been?

"You might say something," she said after a moment. "Aren't we on speaking terms?"

He felt a wisecrack rise to his lips, but held it back. He felt an exquisite sense of shock, not at what he saw, but at what he had never seen before. Cathy was an enchanted thing. She had risen out of the old scalloped bathtub like a beautiful genie.

"Perhaps I'd better go back and come in again," she said.

"Jesus," he said. "Don't move."

"I've never worn this before. It's quite indecent, isn't it?"

Their eyes steadied and picked up the conversation. His resolutions shattered like so much outdated bric-a-brac. His pulse had begun to pound and he let it pound. Her eyes were burnished and in that moment he saw the clear reflection of his own quickening emotions. Their pretenses faded. He slipped his fingers through the sash and pulled her gently to him and kissed her lips.

"You're a magnificent creature," he said. "I guess I've been a fool."

"The door is open."

"Maybe you'd better shut it."

She slipped away and the kimono moved with her like a perfume. Her movements had a superb flow, a restrained urgency that reminded him of a figure on a Chinese screen come to life. She reached the door and the China sun animated the vaulting wedge of space between her legs. She slipped the bolt in place and turned with a quick seriousness in her eyes.

"You mustn't think I planned this, Tom. I *did* want to shock you, but—"

"*Ai-tsai*," he whispered. "She chatters like a gust of wind."

He walked slowly toward her and he hoped he was smiling a little. Motes swirled in the shafts of porthole sun on either side of her. He snapped the short curtains across the ports and the cabin darkened.

"I don't intend to marry you, Tom."

"I don't intend to ask you."

He felt the coolness of silk under his fingertips. She slipped away and shut Koxinga in the bathroom. Wilder held her against the door and she looked up smiling now. It was a smile made of pride and awareness. Their lips met again and he felt himself embraced by a cloud of silk as her arms found his back.

They whispered. They smiled and the moments flowed with a searching, swelling hunger. Cathy's shoulders appeared above the silk, white and luminous in the intimate gloom of the cabin. This isn't the same, Wilder told himself. This kid isn't someone you go to bed with. She's someone you love. Why have I been kidding myself? I'm in love with Cathy. Maybe I've been in love with her since that first dawn on the landing at Chiku Shan.

"Cathy—"

"You will put me off near Swatow, won't you?"

The words, so gently whispered, went through him with an icy current. His shoulders stiffened.

She found his hand and started toward the bunk, but he stopped her. Their eyes met again, but it was different.

"So that's it," he said.

"Tom—"

"Bunk me now and Swatow tomorrow."

"But—"

"Trade. Bargain. Grow up, baby."

"Tom, I only meant—"

He pulled the kimono up over her bare shoulders and crossed the neck tightly across her breasts. His jaws were tight and he could feel the sweat pebbling his forehead. "No sale."

The coffee was boiling over in the pantry. He picked up the blanket and walked out.

He awoke on the pilothouse deck with Cathy's urgent voice in his ears.

"Tom, *quick!*"

He sat up stiffly with her hands still on his shoulders. There was alarm in the air and he felt it at once. The fine-edged anger he'd gone to bed with passed out of importance. The sun had passed to the other side of the islet and the wheelhouse lay in cool shadow. His first glance took in the clock: four-twenty.

"Tom, they've spotted a plane from the hill."

He pulled away and got uncertainly to his feet. "Where?"

"South of us. Zigzagging slowly. It must be out searching for us."

"All right." His skin crawled at the thought of a plane. It hadn't occurred to him to camouflage the weather decks.

He went through the door and started aft. The bluff

cut off half the sky and he saw nothing but the near birds circling for scraps of food. Could they shoot down the plane? Fine chance with their consumptive old guns. The pilot would radio their position at the first burst.

The distant hum of the engine came vibrating through the squawk of birds. Reconnaissance plane, he thought. Probably out of Swatow.

"Knock off those guns!" Wilder shouted. "Sit tight!" Dark faces along the decks below were turned fearfully toward the southern sky. How far was the plane—four or five miles? Wilder glanced at the shocking brightness of the hurricane deck. There might be time....

His eyes flashed at the bird-jacketed rocks and bluffs. "Break out any food you can find! Quickly! Fish, meat—everything. What are you waiting for down there? *K'uai-k'uai!* Spread the word! Scatter food—rice—everything you can lay hands on! Cover the open decks—bow—stern—the paddle wheel!"

They looked up from the decks as if he had gone mad.

"*K'uai-pan!*" he shouted, gesturing with his arms. "Scatter food for the birds! Drag it up here! Goddamn it, get moving!" He wheeled on Cathy. "You've got stuff in the pantry. What are you waiting for?"

"I cooked you a chicken."

"Feed it to the birds."

He slipped down the ladders and invaded the saloon. "Get your food on deck. Quickly, cousins! Spread it around the open decks! Do you understand? Quickly!"

Wilder picked up a basket of rice and carried it astern. He collared a villager and had him start scattering it across the paddle wheel. The birds began to flock in almost at once, screaming and wheeling at the feast being suddenly laid out. Birds awoke from their nests and perches all over the island and the sky darkened with them.

Wilder could no longer hear the plane. He hoped it might be taking a leg toward the mainland, but it would damned well be back. He helped throw food across the hurricane deck—dried fish, fresh vegetables from the crates, chunks of pork. He tossed food onto the pilothouse roof and pandemonium closed in over the *Chiku Shan*. The birds clustered in like bees, surging black and white and gray wings, pink eyes, open beaks; cormorants and fish hawks and gulls. Wilder met Cathy and they beat their way into the shelter of the pilothouse.

There was nothing to do now but wait.

Wilder pulled up the windows. "There's your dinner," he said.

A huge gray pelican sat on the jack staff with a chicken in its caw. Fights began and feathers flew. Birds shrieked and pressed themselves against the glass.

"It's got to work, Tom."

"We must be covered. The pilot may figure a dead whale washed ashore here."

"You do think fast, don't you?"

"Sure, and we'll probably all starve to death before we reach Hong Kong. That plane had better hurry. The feast won't last forever and we'll begin to show in spots."

It grew hot and smelly in the pilothouse; the ship lay under a fluttering blanket of wings.

"Goddamn that plane! Why doesn't it come?" The clock ticked off the seconds.

Suddenly the windows began to buzz in their frames. The plane was zagging over the Brothers. Wilder met Cathy's glance and neither of them moved. It occurred to Wilder suddenly that if the plane came in too low the birds would scatter in fright.

The buzz in the windows rose. Wilder wished he could see out. Was the pilot coming in for a closer look? A gull beat his way along the windows with a dried river fish clipped between its waxy jaws. Cathy stood stiff-shouldered and both of them began to stare at the roof as if they could see through it.

The window buzz softened to a hum.

Still they waited, fearing the plane might come about for a closer look and disrobe them.

The windows fell silent except for the brushing of wings.

"He's not coming back," Wilder said finally.

Cathy's shoulders fell and she took a breath. "That oafish pelican," she muttered. "I wish I'd put curry on the chicken to burn his throat."

Chapter Twenty

Wilder first noticed a fall in the barometer at nine that night.

Clouds had come scudding up from the southwest at twilight. Under a streaked rose and lavender sky Wilder had backed the *Chiku Shan* past the reef and been willing to risk the first obscured hours of moonlight. He had hoped to grind eighty miles out of the creaking old ferryboat during the next eleven hours, and once the reef was behind them he had stepped up to full speed.

It had taken better than an hour to beat off the birds and wash down the ship. A few were caught, their stomachs slit, and chunks of pork and even whole river fish reclaimed. A dozen catties of rice had been spared, there were fowl and animals for slaughter, and there was sugar cane. Still, the village appetite would go through small mountains of food each day and a rationing system had already been organized. And there was wood to be got for the voracious boiler furnace. They would be out of fuel by morning.

Now, some three hours southwest of the Brothers, Wilder glanced again at the grimy Japanese barometer. Could he trust the damned thing? If a storm were brewing he ought to steam for the coast and hunt shelter before it was too late. Their flat-bottomed river boat would be no match for a roiling sea and they'd consume their fuel fighting it.

They stood on a course for Lamock Island, with its lighthouse to set a new course by. The rocky indentation with Swatow at its center stretched some fifty miles wide, he remembered, and he wanted to be well clear of it by morning. He had been unable to straighten out in his mind the complexity of islands and shifting sand knolls, and preferred to avoid all its dangers.

The compass had lied—why not the barometer as well? Some twenty miles off the coast, they had already begun to parallel the gaping Swatow indentation. The thought of turning shoreward on the advice of a delicate and possibly faulty instrument was bitter and irksome. How had the glass covering its face been cracked? Had the barometer been dropped?

Was a storm coming or not?

To hell with it, he decided firmly. He'd stay on course unless they were chased off it. Every hour they remained in the Strait of Formosa left them vulnerable; he wasn't going to hang around waiting for a storm dreamed up by a crackpot barometer. They had eighty miles to cover that night.

Cathy brought him something to eat and he saw that she felt no remorse or embarrassment over the affair that morning in the cabin. He was no longer sure that she had deliberately planned the silken trap for him; he tried to believe she had been honestly caught up in her own sudden desires. Nevertheless, some part of her mind had remained cool enough to recognize a final opportunity to get her way, and Swatow had slipped off her tongue. He was glad he had walked out and tried now to forget the whole miserable affair. But he knew he hadn't left the cabin the same man who had walked in. He was damned well in love with her, he had found that out, and he hadn't been able to shut the door on it. Well, he was sorry. He had no business falling in love with Cathy. It was absurd.

She remained in the wheelhouse until almost midnight. She chattered. She was bright and vibrant and entirely at ease, and he liked having her around, even when she chattered. She asked questions, tried her hand at the big wheel, and got the hang of it quickly.

"Old Mr. Feng has finally stopped his awful weeping," she said, her legs spread at the helm. "Am I doing this right?"

"You're doing swell." He relaxed at the chart table and was glad for the relief. His calves were aching again; he was no longer used to long stretches on his feet. The dim sight of Cathy at the big oak wheel, her legs apart, her arms outstretched, amused him. She seemed entirely sure of herself; but of course, he thought, that was Cathy.

"I didn't know he was weeping," Wilder said. "He was merely seasick the last time I went by."

"He wasn't seasick. He thought his gold had been left behind in the village. Blubbery hysterics. Mr. Tso finally got around to explaining that his greasy fortune was aboard."

"And now he's happy."

"Fixed him up like a tonic."

There was other news. One of the Han women had had her first labor pains—the baby was coming early. Susu's grief had been overwhelmed by seasickness; she hadn't eaten a thing since Amoy and wanted to die.

Despite his efforts to ignore it, Wilder couldn't keep his eyes off the barometer. It continued to fall. *Maybe it means we're in for a hot spell*, he thought angrily.

"One more thing," Cathy said. "I'm moving out of your cabin. I don't intend to let you sleep up here on the floor."

"Deck."

"Whatever it is."

"Where do you intend moving to?"

"There's always room in the saloon with Susu."

"But no bathtub for Koxinga."

She hesitated; suddenly she changed her tactics. "Tom, you were awfully sweet this morning, but you needn't be noble about it. Look, I'm grown up now. I can look out for myself. There's no reason we can't share the cabin. I like—sort of keeping house for you."

"All right," he said softly. "If that's the way you want it."

"I do—really."

He was alone in the pilothouse when they headed into the squall. Was this the advance guard of a storm moving up from the south? Rain swept over them in a jingling shower, rattling the windows and turning the jack staff into a wavering yellow shape before him. Wilder had an impulse to streak for shore. The roof came alive with the rattling of heavy raindrops and Wilder saw the bow strike up its first explosion of spray. He stiffened at the wheel.

The door flew open and a wet shape entered the cabin.

"There is a note for you, Captain."

"Who are you?"

"I guard Old Feng. He tell me quick carry this note to you."

The ship bucked a swell and the flat bottom slapped the sea with a loud swack. The wheel was jerked out of Wilder's hand.

"Get out of here!"

He caught the grips and knew he'd lost the gamble. The barometer had been telling the truth.

"But, Captain—"

"I said clear out!"

A clap of wind shook a wooden moan from the bulkheads. Wilder had been piloting through a fool's paradise. He cursed his arrogance in the face of the barometer. They were in for it. The storm had speed under her windy skirts. It was too late to reverse course and attempt to run ahead of it.

"It is of importance, this note, Captain."

"Are you deaf? *Kun-pa!*"

"He goes nowhere."

It was a new voice. The door on the port side jerked open and Wilder awakened to a new situation. He swung the wheel to hold the bows in the wind, but his mind raced in a different direction. He was getting company on both sides. Three men.

Squeeze play.

For a moment the impact of the storm was forgotten. There was a heavy thud at Wilder's feet as Old Feng's guard was sapped to the deck; he hadn't been a phony. It was all Wilder could do to keep his hands on the fighting wheel as the two men closed in on either side of him.

"All right," Wilder said sharply. "You're a couple of

BLOOD ALLEY

Red Fengs."

"That's right, foolish captain."

The deck tilted as the ferry bucked again and dug water out of the sea. Foam raced as white as starch along the main deck. The man on Wilder's left was thrown back, but got to his feet quickly. Wilder didn't dare let go of the wheel; the ferry would drift about and start taking the storm broadside.

"All right, what do you want?"

"This vessel belongs to the People, yes? What right have you to take what belongs to the People?"

"Never mind the knuckle-rapping."

"We take command now. You do what we say. You will change direction. You will take us into Swatow."

"No kidding."

The wind was picking up a shriek from the guy wires and another blast came crashing in, twisting the upper decks in the hog frames. The swells were building up under them and Wilder knew that if they took one broadside they'd be swamped. It would be committing suicide to change course.

"Go to hell," Wilder snapped.

"You will do as we command."

"Get out of here—both of you."

Wilder felt the point of a knife in his back. His hands remained helplessly glued to the wheel. The other Feng rapped his arm with a capstan bar.

"We give orders now, foolish captain. Not you."

"Your grandfather will be killed," Wilder said. "He'll be torn apart."

"We think not." It was the man on his left that did the talking; an indefinite shape with a thick, self-assured voice. "No one knows until we see the lights of Swatow what has happened. By then it will be too late for such violence—and very stupid. Now you will change course."

The flat bottom slapped water again, racking the spine of the ship. An hour of this, Wilder thought, and they'd be driftwood.

He fought to keep a calm voice. "If I refuse?"

"You will not refuse, running dog!" the other Feng spat, and Wilder felt the restrained smack of the capstan bar against his shoulder muscle.

"No," the other said in steadier tones. "You will not refuse unless you wish us to strip the skin off your back as you stand there."

"You know what they'll do to your fellow villagers in Swatow?"

"The unworthy pigs will get what they deserve. They insult the People of China with their criminal flight. Our family has been kidnaped, and for that too they must pay. Quickly—do as we command!"

"You crazy bastards, we can't take this storm broadside." The point of the knife ripped through Wilder's shirt, opening skin as it went. Wilder's back stiffened. He thought of the open voice tubes. Was Tack able to hear any of this down in the engine room? He just as quickly abandoned any hope of it, and wondered if he dared let go of the wheel long enough to murder these guys.

"You'll sink us."

"Don't try to fool us, stupid captain."

The bell over Wilder's head jingled recklessly in the swinging pilothouse. The wind, stiffening every moment, flattened itself against the windows.

"Still you delay?"

Wilder drove the wheel hard to starboard; he wasn't going to stand there and let them skin him alive. He'd risk playing their game for a few dangerous broadside moments.

"*Hao, hao!*" The burning knife came away.

The bows began coming around and the Fengs began

to mutter to themselves. "He spoke of a note from our grandfather."

"Let us see."

The note was taken out of the fist of the prone village guard under match light. Wilder got his first glance at the new command. They were half pints, both of them, with black, expressionless eyes. The man with the match, the capstan bar hooked under his arm, had long Confucian ears and eyebrows like powder burns.

The first broadside swell caught them and the pilothouse swung madly. The wind drove against them even as they settled in the trough; a guy wire snapped and went screaming through the wind. The turnbuckle struck wood with a splintering blow. Wilder felt the new sag in the hurricane deck under his feet. This was madness.

Suddenly he realized that the man with the knife was no longer behind him. He could be heard from the doorway emptying his guts.

Seasick.

Wilder's hands left the wheel and he sprang for the other Feng as the match went out.

"*Ai!*"

Wilder was an instant too late. The Red nephew had got a grip on the capstan bar and Wilder felt it across his cheek. But there hadn't been time to cock it and Wilder was unhurt. He swung through blackness and connected with flesh, and then the flesh vanished.

The wheelhouse pitched wildly and the sea crashed over the bow. The helm went creaking in a spin like a carnival wheel. Suddenly the capstan cracked Wilder's ankle with almost enough force to break it and Wilder dived where he thought the little guy must be. He was.

Wilder got hold of the man's shirt and bounced his

head against the deck. He caught a struggling arm, paralyzed it, and wrenched the bar free. At the same moment he found the seasick Feng on his back. He pitched him off and the Feng under him backwatered. Suddenly he screamed and a rapid thud came from the helm. The idiot must have backed his head into the spinning oak grips. Wilder swung the capstan, struck flesh, and thought he heard the knife clatter across the deck. He swung again. He waited.

But the fight was over.

Pain had erupted from Wilder's right ankle; now he felt it. Blood from his open back had reached his trousers. He felt his way past the wheel and whistled down the voice tube.

"Chief engineer!"

Tack was a long time in coming.

"We take water, Captain."

"Is it bad?"

"Not yet."

"Get someone up here. There's been a fight."

"What?"

"Bodies on the floor! I want them cleared out."

He left the tube impatiently and pulled the Feng out from under the wheel. He waited until the ship sank to the bottom of a trough and regained the wheel. It took all the muscle he had to bring her over and head her back into the storm; he wanted to put one foot on the wheel, but he felt one-legged. His right ankle had turned to fire.

The bows tore a patch out of an oncoming swell and the flat bottom crashed, shaking the bulkheads. Tack and one of his firemen appeared with a flashlight and took in the damage. In the beam of light Wilder saw that the long-eared Feng had got his face pulped in the ripsaw of the wheel grips. The other was no longer conscious of his stomach. The capstan bar had sent him sprawling. There was the blood of three men smeared across the wheelhouse linoleum.

"You are hurt, Captain," Tack muttered, holding the light to Wilder's back.

Wilder glowered. "Just get these punks out from underfoot. How are you doing on fuel?"

"We don't worry yet. And we will still float with a stomach full of water." The bodies were roughly pulled out of Wilder's way and Tack sent his fireman for another hand.

"Go easy on that one," Wilder said. "He's not a part of it. One of Old Feng's guards."

"What happened?"

Wilder gave the story in a few clipped sentences. The ferry rose over a swell that left the paddle wheel spinning free in the air. They came down on their flat belly and the woodwork groaned in all its aching joints. But Wilder's spirits began to rise. The old lady was still in her corset of guy wires and hog frames and Tack seemed only mildly concerned with the weather. They were far from driftwood yet and they were taking the storm on their bows, where it belonged.

The wheelhouse bell tinkled stupidly.

"As soon as this fish pond begins to behave," Tack said, "we'll round up the other men of their family. Now there aren't six of us aboard who aren't seasick. It will have to wait."

Tack returned to his machinery. The fireman and another villager brought Cathy into the pilothouse, lit the lantern, and hung it overhead. She wore a yellow robe that had been drenched in the short trip up the outside ladder, and her hair clung to her head.

"Kill the lantern," Wilder said.

"Leave it on," Cathy said firmly. The lantern continued to circle from its hook and the fireman removed the bodies. The rain and the sea had begun to collect into shifting puddles, washing in and out under the pilothouse doors.

Cathy ripped open the back of Wilder's shirt as he stood at the wheel, favoring his right leg. She studied the slice in his back, and the next moment she set it on fire.

"Iodine," she said. "Probably the last bottle in China. Aren't you lucky?"

"My middle name."

She dressed the wound despite Wilder's movements at the wheel and examined his ankle. The sea was getting worse and they pitched around like a cork. Finally Wilde got Tack on the voice tube again.

"Is there any oil aboard?"

"Perhaps twenty gallons for lubricating."

Wilder cursed his wood-burning ship. The ferry was going to break her spine taking these sprawling belly flops. He ought to be pouring oil over the swells to make a slick to windward and calm their bed.

"Never mind. Forget it."

Cathy taped his ankle and taped a gash across his cheek he hadn't known was there.

"Your ankle's probably sprained," she said. "You ought to go to bed."

"Thanks."

"It should have cold packs around it."

"I'll send the boy out for some ice cubes."

Cathy finally killed the lantern and he was glad to get the window glare out of his eyes. It surprised him, some three hours later, to discover that she was still in the wheelhouse with him.

The jack staff sliced the gale in two. The ferryboat splashed and groaned and shook herself. Finally the jack staff cracked off and came swinging through the air. It hit one of the port windows and shot exploding glass around them.

Rain swirled into the pilothouse, but Wilder was beyond caring. She ought to have split up long ago, he thought. What was holding her together? A final gust of wind would tear the pilothouse out by its roots, and that would be the end of it.

At four o'clock the swells began to level and the wind died to a moan. There was only the rain, splashing down with a softer touch, as if it were trying to make friends.

Chapter Twenty-one

Wilder stood unblinking at the wheel, his right foot in a bucket of cold water.

Where the hell were they?

Rain thickened the gray, brooding dawn. Listing slightly to port, as if driven by a wind that wasn't there, the *Chiku Shan* felt her way through the rain-pocked sea, her paddle wheel thrashing at half speed to save fuel. It became an effort for Wilder to blink his eyes; his lids felt as if they were starched open. His ankle had swollen. Once the sea was flattened, Cathy had got a bucket of icy water from the depths and made him stand in it.

Wilder had to find land before the vaporous clouds lifted. The morning had become something in slow motion; even the creaking of bruised wood about him was tempered and restrained.

Tack's voice, remarkably fresh and powerful, came whistling up from the engine room. "Awake up there?"

Wilder leaned across to the voice tube. "Good morning, chief engineer."

"Can you see land yet?"

"We can't see more than eight hundred yards."

"Look for a nest to roost in, Captain. I have not more

than a cord of wood left in the bins."

"Drop speed again."

"At most, we steam another hour and a quarter."

"All right."

Wilder straightened awkwardly and cursed the bucket on his foot. He scanned the low, misty sea again. What the devil was their position? How far from the mainland? Thirty miles? They should have passed the Lamock Island light hours ago, but it hadn't shown up through the storm, if it stood where he had charted it at all. How far off course had the swells driven them? He remembered the way the Swatow coast dropped back, which would put them even farther at sea with one cord of wood in the bins. Still, he hesitated to cut off to starboard. He couldn't shake the feeling that the city of Swatow itself must be somewhere abeam of them and they might feel their way through the rain right up alongside the customs pier, burning all the furniture aboard to get there. And that would be the crowning absurdity.

Cathy returned to the pilothouse with a fresh pot of tea and a stub of a broom. "You're going to give your ankle some rest," she said. "Give me a moment to sweep up this mess. Even I can hold up that wheel in this kind of sea. Your foot's had an awful bang and it's not going to get any better if you go on standing on it."

"You can deep-six this bucket of water. I'm through swimming. Where's Big Han?"

"He's been seasick for hours."

Wilder would be glad to get off the wheel. He wanted to go over his chart and figure out a new course. Cathy got busy with the broom, sweeping up broken glass and water.

"Move."

She swept around his feet and stopped to pick up a

scrap of paper drying against the base of the compass binnacle.

"Is this anything you want?"

Wilder glanced down. Was that the note Old Feng's guard had come up with? "Read it."

She straightened on the broom and studied the smeared Chinese characters. Finally she read it to him. "'Illustrious Grandfather: Do not fear for your life. Tonight, when the ship sleeps, we take command. Tomorrow you will awake in Swatow and safety.'" She looked up. "Where did this come from?"

He had forgotten the message; now it was only a footnote to the miserable little affair with the bloody little Fengs.

"The two heroes must have smuggled that to Old Feng last night. He sent it up here to warn me. I was too busy to listen."

"I still don't understand. Old Feng wouldn't—"

"Apparently he would. Now that he knows his money's aboard, maybe he's all for deserting the People's Republic, even if it means sacrificing a pair of nephews to the tenth power in the bargain. I suppose he's on our side now, if we want him."

"He's despicable."

"Aren't you finished sweeping?"

She finally took the wheel and the *Chiku Shan* went leaning through the rain. Wilder managed to get his sandal back on and poured himself a cup of tea at the chart table. He began to study the map. But he found it difficult to concentrate. He listened to the tired straining of the ship and felt something more than an embarrassed affection for this strange little ferry he commanded. He would never get used to the splash of the paddle wheel, but it was no longer a ridiculous sound in his ears. The old river boat hadn't been designed for the sea. Still, she had taken the thrashing.

She felt loose and disjointed, but she was still afloat. He had misused her and the barometer still hung with its cracked leering face to remind him of it.

Cathy broke into his thoughts. "The animal pens got torn away last night."

"What?"

"I was just down there. The pigs are gone. Fortunately, the goats were tethered, and they're still with us. Poor things are half drowned. The fowl got washed overboard, too."

Wilder turned. "How much food is there left aboard?"

"I don't know."

Wilder returned dismally to his chart and tried not to think of the pigs and chickens and ducks trying to stay afloat in the storm.

He had indicated a broken hurdle of islands stretching from Lamock westward through Namoa to the mainland. Only a miracle would have got the ferry through this graveyard during the storm. Either they had not yet reached Lamock, which seemed impossible, or had passed to the east of it. He chose the latter possibility; they couldn't have blundered through that fence of islands.

Well, that put them several hours out from the mainland with an hour's wood in the bins.

He fixed his estimated position and studied the mainland coast below Swatow. He had marked Hope Bay with a danger area of detached rocks lying off the western shore and wondered if it would offer some cove to hide in for the day, if they could reach it. These rain clouds weren't going to sit on their shoulders all day, he thought.

He had a vague memory of low sandy beaches between the cape at Hope Bay and the point, and decided against the area as too open. His eyes moved south a few miles to Haimun Bay, and he could see the reef standing like bangles from the headland. It stood farther from the seaport and he thought it a more promising target. He estimated a thirty-degree error in the compass and decided on a new course to the southwest.

He hobbled back to the wheel and helped Cathy swing it about to the new bearing. He felt the touch of her shoulders against his outstretched arm. Her hands dropped and she turned slowly within his arms, putting her back to the wheel, and looked up at him.

"Hello, Tom."

"The course," he said, "is three-o-five."

"You were majestic last night. I watched you."

"Knock it off, baby."

She stood caged by his arms, an irresolute smile in her eyes. He disliked the moment. His thoughts were rooted to the chart, to the shortages of fuel and food, and he hated the word majestic.

"Last night I found out for sure, Tom."

"What are you trying to say?"

"I'm in love with you. Maybe it really started a long me ago. I don't know. I—"

His eyes lowered and met her dark stare. "All right," he said doubtfully. "You're in love with me."

"You don't want me to be, do you? You don't want anyone to be in love with you, do you?"

"Now that we understand each other, maybe you'd better get out of here."

Wilder's hands were moist on the wheel. She couldn't be serious. Sure, he was in love with her, but that was his business. He wasn't the type that well-bred English girls fell in love with. The storm had put her emotions through the wringer and now there was an unfamiliar earnestness about her. Well, she was right—he didn't want her to be in love with him. She would wake up in Hong Kong and see him for what he was, a man in the crowd, indistinguishable and easily forgotten.

He wasn't going to let himself in for that.

"The truth is," she muttered softly, "I didn't really like you very much at first. I'm not sure I want to be in love with you, but I am, Tom. I'm sorry if you don't want it."

"Cathy—"

"Please don't say it. I can see that noble look coming into your eyes, and I despise it." Her manner stiffened and she turned back to take the wheel. "What did you say our course is?"

He was glad to leave his thoughts unsaid. He was no good at moments like this, and he'd only make matters worse. He left her at the wheel and hobbled out of the pilothouse for a quick look at the ship's damage.

He stood for a moment in the rain splashing down on the hurricane deck and wondered if they could possibly hold together another couple of hundred miles. Two broken guy wires swayed from the hog post, leaving the after section of the deck to sag. At least one of the guys had its turnbuckle and maybe there was a chance for minor repair. He eased himself down the ladder and saw that a ten-foot section of the saloon-deck guardrail had been ripped out.

The ship had the quiet air of a derelict, the decks leaning and deserted, the cabin doors shut. If all the passengers were seasick, they wouldn't be hungry, and that was something to the credit side.

He opened the saloon door and the twittering of canaries met him. There were Chinese bundled up all over the deck and only a few signs of life. He saw Mr. Tso and two others aft, where the kitchen had been, attempting to regain order out of the fallen pots and pans and spilled rice.

"We're running out of fuel," Wilder explained. "Better

have some of this furniture broken up and taken down to the furnace."

The elder straightened and Wilder had never seen him look so old. "It would be a pity. Much of this wood is treasured. You see this?" He pointed to a nearby three-part blackwood screen, fluttering with carved birds and coiling dragons. "Perhaps the artist gave ten years of his life to this scrap of wood. It would be a pity to turn it to ashes."

"I'm sorry."

"Yes. Perhaps it must be."

Wilder saw Susu lying near a stanchion and spent a moment trying to cheer her up. She smiled wanly and he moved on.

The cargo deck was bare except for the three frightened goats tethered aft of the boiler room. There were scraps of broken wood about, the lacquered leg of a chair, a broken fragment of gingerbread hanging from the deck above, banging against a rail stanchion. Wilder hobbled through the area where the animal pens had been, picking up what loose wood he could find. He saw the lifeboat dangling from a single davit, like a broken limb. Well, that would burn too.

An hour later the *Chiku Shan's* funnel smoke came from a rich diet of carved chests and tables and screens. Cathy remained stubbornly at the wheel. If he wouldn't go to bed with his ankle, he could stretch out on the pilothouse bench. He decided not to argue with her and let her keep the helm. She couldn't have hit land if she tried.

Some two hours later Tack climbed into the pilothouse, his face marked with grease and disintegrating hope in his apricot eyes. "There is land yet?"

Wilder roused himself from the bench. "Not yet."

"The furniture goes quickly. It was a trifle. Most

washed away from the cargo deck last night."

"See if you can get Big Han to his feet and have him organize a party to take off the cabin doors."

"Your leg is bad, eh?"

"They can also strip the gingerbread, even though I don't suppose it'll give you much fire."

"I want to burn the coffins, but the old man refuses. He speaks of one of God's footsteps. He says we have only to be patient. Bah!"

"What did your firemen do with the Feng boys?"

"They make no more trouble for us."

"Are they aboard?"

Tack wiped his face, smiling faintly. "No, Captain. They wanted to go to Swatow. All right. We point them to Swatow and tell them, 'Swim comrades.'"

Cathy barely flinched.

At nine-thirty the paddle wheel seemed to explode behind them. Wilder jumped up to ring off speed and hobbled aft across the hurricane deck. Splintered ribs of wood floated in their spreading wake, together with the water-soaked log they had run over.

The paddle wheel settled into silence, its chest broken.

Chapter Twenty-two

At noon the *Chiku Shan* lay helplessly in the Strait.

Li the carpenter labored in unruffled patience at the broken cage of the wheel. Wilder shook villagers out of their seasickness to man the machine guns and put a lookout on the roof of the pilothouse. He ordered complete silence. The floating log led him to believe they were nearer shore than he had thought; fishing junks or other boats might be in the area, rain or not.

"Tom, I'm terribly sorry. I simply didn't see any log."

"It might happen to me next time. Don't worry about it."

The lifeboat had gone into the furnace and it had been impossible to chase down the paddle fragments in the sea. The carpenter, his small craftsman's eyes surveying the damage, forgot his seasickness and muttered precise orders to his apprentice, equally green around the eyes and uncertain on his legs.

Wilder remained aft for the first dismal hour. There were ten long buckets to the wheel and six of them had been snapped. Li returned from the boiler room with what lumber and materials he thought he could use: a complete warped mahogany door, a section of guardrail, a pocketful of bolts. Chips began to fly in the rain.

Wilder was soaking wet. It was only after he saw the first new paddle bolted in place that he could bring himself to leave. His leg felt numb and he cursed the Fengs all the way back to the Shang dynasty. He saw fishing nets and floats being put over the side and hoped the delay would be good for something. The big wheel would never be the same, but maybe Li would get it to dig water.

A dizzy spell had come, but Wilder had shaken it off.

The junk appeared through the rain shortly before two o'clock.

The alarm spread and Wilder went to the starboard doorway. A moment later Cathy climbed up to the pilothouse. He saw a great, finlike sail take shape abeam of them.

It cut slowly through the rain. Fishing junk, Wilder thought. A dog on its poop deck began to bark at them across the sea. The junk tacked, steered aft of the paddle-wheeler, and silently swung around. The machine gunners followed it. The junk, staying a few hundred yards out, circled the *Chiku Shan* like a buzzard eying carrion.

Silently it vanished again through the heavy curtain of rain.

"What do you suppose *that* means?" Cathy muttered.

"I don't know. Something kept him at a distance."

"Do you suppose the alarm's been spread along the coast to watch for us?"

"I doubt it. The Reds won't want to advertise our break. It might put ideas in other heads."

"Well, he's gone. Look, you *must* get off that leg. You ought to be in bed."

He left her standing and worked his way painfully to the paddle wheel. Neither Li nor his apprentice was there.

He found them in the boiler room, scavenging for more wood.

"How much longer?"

Li stopped to wipe his bony face. "We have trouble to find wood five *ch'ih* long for the wheel."

"You have two more paddles to put in."

"Yes. Maybe three hours' work."

Wilder knew it was useless to ask them to speed it up. They understood the danger the ship was in, but Li was a craftsman and he wouldn't be hurried. Wilder hobbled away.

He ordered Tack to build up steam in the boiler again. "There is little to burn, Captain. You want to keep warm, it is better to drink tea."

Wilder didn't feel like arguing. There had been something malevolent in the way the junk had swung around them, watching, and Wilder wanted some pressure. "There's plenty of wood. If we have to, we'll put the ship in the furnace, deck by deck, right down to the scuppers. Build up your fire."

When half an hour had passed and nothing changed but the pressure in the boiler, Wilder began to doubt the wisdom of wasting fuel. The day was passing and a dark night for travel stood ahead of them once the wheel was fixed. He scanned the surrounding waters and precious wood went up in smoke. Maybe he'd been a fool to get rattled by that junk.

Cathy returned to the pilothouse with a bowl of soup. He didn't have the chance to eat it.

A shout went up from the bow and almost at once the machine gun started clacking. Wilder jumped back to the window and the other three guns aboard picked up the rattle, spitting their fire to starboard.

"What is it, Tom?"

The rain had parted in a dozen places and a fleet of junks came silently through the gloom.

Wilder hobbled across the pilothouse for his gun. "That goddamned junk went back to tip off the pack. Get aft and tell the carpenters to stay clear of the wheel."

"But—"

"Hurry up!"

He rang the engine room to stand by, and dropped one of the windows. Sure, Wilder thought, we look like easy plunder even to a bunch of fishermen. Four old peashooters to keep them off with. Great.

"Aim lower! Never mind chewing up their sails! Shoot for the decks!"

The junks, their wooden eyes glowering with paint, were spreading out to encircle the *Chiku Shan* in the rain. Part-time buccaneers, he thought bitterly, fishermen with the South China taste for piracy.

The air chattered, and then the bow gun jammed. The fishing fleet kept tightening its circle, ignoring the bee stings, holding its fire!

And then it let go. A window shattered somewhere

under the pilothouse. Wilder took aim, following a Chinese at his tiller, and squeezed the trigger. He saw the man drop and searched through the rain for another target. He emptied his gun and hoped Cathy had reached the paddle wheel to warn the carpenters out of the way. He wasn't going to sit there and let the ferryboat be boarded.

He hit the bell and got on the voice tube, "Let's get out of here! Full speed ahead!"

There was no answer from the voice tube and he gave the bell signal again. He didn't know how much speed they could get with a seven-foot gap in the paddle wheel, but he was going to find out.

The piston began to stroke. A piece of lead came whining through the open pilothouse door and sang against the compass binnacle at Wilder's feet. The paddle wheel began to thrash. The bow jarred and moved.

Wilder grabbed the wheel.

"Rake the decks!" he shouted through the open window. "Get your fire down! You're not doing any good!"

Where the hell did they learn to shoot?

He steered for a weathered junk dead ahead; he could feel the gap in their propulsion, but they were damned well moving. Funnel smoke blackened the rain about them. The *Chiku Shan* raised a sudden confusion in the war dance of junks around it. Wilder saw the circle began to break apart and then two junks collided, their masts and nets flopping over each other. Below him, the bow machine gun was barking fire again.

The junk ahead lifted its skirts to get out of the way and the two ships passed within twenty yards of each other, lead flying. A slug caught the bucket on the pilothouse floor and Wilder was glad his leg hadn't been in it.

The ferryboat went crashing through the wooden chain into the open sea, and almost as suddenly as it had come the chatter of gunfire died.

The stern-wheeler charged forward like an automobile with missing spark plugs, full of hesitations and vibrations. But they got out of there.

Chapter Twenty-three

They spotted the wreck shortly after five o'clock.

Wilder steered for it cautiously, wary of submerged rocks. The masts and bowsprit of an old schooner rose stiffly through the thinning rain. She lay at a tilt, her stern down, and water eddied around the deckhouse.

She was all wood.

Wilder searched his mind for some glimmer of recognition; if he could place the wreck, he would know his position. He steered along the leeward side, corning in close, thankful for the *Chiku Shan's* shallow draft. He rang off speed. The tire fenders squealed as the two ships touched and Big Han jumped aboard the sloping deck to tie up.

Wilder remained at the wheel, trying to wipe a dizzy spell out of his eyes. The pain in his ankle was shooting to his hip. His head cleared and he watched as villagers went over the side with their tools, spreading across the wreck like hungry animals. They had an hour's daylight to strip wood from the wreck for the *Chiku Shan's* furnace. It struck Wilder as cannibalism for one ship to be feeding on another.

He turned to his chart. His vision kept blurring and he cursed himself. Where was this wreck? It looked old and wave-beaten; it must have been hung up years ago. He turned suddenly as someone entered the wheelhouse.

Mr. Tso.

He came bearing gifts. "My people ask me to show our feelings. So. Quite so. This gentle lark to sing to you." He hung the cage from a hook above. "A bottle of rice wine."

"Thank your people."

"They worry about our eminent brother." With his hands empty, Mr. Tso tugged at his beard, and Wilder saw that he had lost his comb from its ribbon. "He is in pain. He must have rest. Perhaps we can stop where we are."

Wilder began to sense something behind Mr. Tso's gift-bearing visit. Had Cathy gone to him and exaggerated his condition? Now that they were tied up, he'd flake out for an hour. That was all he needed. His ankle wasn't going to heal with a night's sleep and to hell with it.

"I don't think it would be very healthy to remain or even head for shore," Wilder said. "The fishing fleet will be telling everyone about the ferryboat that got away. We haven't put them very far behind."

"It will soon be dark. We have little to fear."

"We travel best at night and there's a lot of wood alongside us. Call it one of God's footsteps, if you want to. We'll stay tied up until Li finishes repairing the wheel and we can take aboard a night's fuel. Then we go."

"My son, it is not necessary to prove your courage to us. We have seen it, and we can be patient."

"I'm not trying to prove anything."

He returned to his chart, and after a moment Mr. Tso left.

Wilder slept an uneasy three hours in the cabin, doorless now, like the others. The cracking and splitting of wood from the lower decks kept rousing him. He had seen one of the schooner's masts come aboard; they'd be able to hack several cords of wood out of the wreck. New hope was something tangible around him. He could hear it in the enthusiasm of the voices and in the quick sounds of footsteps.

His leg throbbed. When he realized that Cathy was in the cabin with him, he wondered if he'd slept at all.

He raised himself on his elbows. "Has the wheel been fixed?"

"It's fixed, Tom."

He threw off his blanket with difficulty and then he felt her hands gently restraining him. "Please, Tom. You can't possibly stay on your feet another night. Be reasonable. We can stay tied up to the wreck."

"Cut it out." He pushed past her and swung his leg around. Did they take him for a kid? He had a sprained ankle and maybe a headful of fatigue and so what? They ought to be able to put themselves sixty or seventy miles nearer Hong Kong by morning. Was she worried because they'd soon be well past Swatow?

The rain had vanished. The night sea stood under a patched roof of clouds.

They got under way again.

Wilder felt better with the wheel in his hands. The thrashing of the paddles behind him was a good sound in his ears and his spirits began to rise. The stern wheel was full of guts and it would shove them all the way to Hong Kong.

Shortly before midnight Wilder was alerted by a faint glow on the western horizon. He stared, blinking to keep his eyes focused. A lighthouse? Which lighthouse? The one around Good Hope Cape, or was that the Breaker Point light? He hadn't been able to place the wrecked schooner and he wished he could catch a bearing to go by. If it was Breaker Point, that meant Tungao Road lay ahead, together with a waiting barricade of rocks—Flat Rock, Korea Rock, Sunk Rock ... He couldn't begin to remember all of them.

He decided to come in for a closer look and turned the wheel. Cathy brought up another pot of tea. If he ever reached Hong Kong, he thought, he'd never look at the stuff again.

"The least you can let me do," she said, "is steer. I couldn't possibly hit another log."

"Later."

She redressed the wound on his back as he stood there. "Hungry?"

"No."

"They've killed two of the goats."

If he could get close enough to spot a steel tower, that would make it Breaker Point, and he would have a bearing.

Two miles out he could see it. Breaker Point! There was the dim white patch that would be the lightkeeper's house and the stiff, latticed framework of the tower. It was all beautifully familiar. He knew where he was.

He swung the wheel to port and leaned out the window.

"Down there, cousins! Watch for rocks!"

He cut speed and was thankful again for the flat bottom under him. He got the light on his beam and his vision swam again. His hands tightened on the wheel, and with Cathy in the pilothouse with him he held his head stiff and finally the dizziness washed away.

The next three miles were anxious and slow. Wilder knew that here the coast wedged back toward a river, and once they were through the off-shore rocks it would be clear steaming for some twenty miles.

His vision began dancing again and this time he

couldn't struggle out of it.

"Tom—what is it?"

A moment later he collapsed.

Chapter Twenty-four

There was the roar of distant surf. Wilder awoke with sunlight speckling the cabin. A gull was wheeling above the ship, casting a broken shadow in and out of the door. The chunking of the paddle wheel had vanished and the ship lay in a weird, lonely silence.

Wilder felt too stiff to move. He saw that his leg lay newly taped, more loosely than before, propped high on an arrangement of folded blankets. He turned in the bunk and gazed at the wrinkled face of land rising beside the doorway, almost close enough to touch. Where the hell were they?

His first fear was that he had hung them up on a rock somewhere off Breaker Point. He eased himself off the bed and discovered that the pain in his leg had drawn back to his ankle. He felt pleasantly cool.

Susu appeared from the pantry and her short fingers went flying.

"What you tly do? Killee self? Clazy Melican! In bed! Chop-chop!"

"Where are we?"

"Ebelyting O.K. My numba-one nurse—you see."

He noticed now that branches and leaves were littered across the passageway. They were camouflaged as before, and he turned back to the amah. "You're looking fine," he said. "We must be on land."

"My fixee soup. You eat. Catchee more sleep."

"Maskee, maskee."

He went into the sun and found the ship entirely shaggy. When he reached the pilothouse he saw that a broad, stumplike islet stood against his cabin doorway.

The mainland cliffs rose sharply up on the other side of them.

He was astonished. The ship had tucked itself under a reddish Chinese cliff, concealed from the Strait by an islet, and there was a mud flat drying under them. Someone had pulled off a sweet piece of piloting.

Well, where was everyone?

"Susu!"

When she came up the pilothouse ladder she carried a bowl of soup stubbornly in her hands.

"Ol ligh!" she snapped impatiently. "My hold you down, makee you eat."

"Just tell me what the hell happened."

"Missy Cathy, she plenty cool head. Walkee fellyboat in here, you bet."

Wilder found that almost impossible to believe; he'd get the story from Tack.

"Now you eat."

"All right. Is everyone on shore leave?"

"Most ebelyone go 'cept old people. Find wood on beach. Maybe buy food. Maybe village somewhere."

Wilder's eyes flashed up from the soup bowl. "Isn't Cathy aboard?"

"She be back. You no wolly."

"When did she leave?"

"One, two hour ago. Soup no good?"

"The soup's fine."

"My clean cabin. You catchee more sleep. Savvy?"

She left finally and Wilder pushed away the soup. Something cold settled in the pit of his stomach. It was crazy. Cathy wouldn't have run off. Yet he couldn't shake a growing fear that she wasn't coming back. He looked at his chart and after a moment decided Swatow couldn't be more than forty miles north of them. Still, she wasn't a complete idiot. She'd got Swatow out of her system, hadn't she?

He limped to the window and gazed vacantly at the tangle of limbs and branches matting the bows. He saw two villagers approaching along the mud flat, their backs piled high with bundles of driftwood for the furnace. The tide was obviously out now and there wasn't enough water under them to wash a pair of socks in.

Why had Cathy gone ashore? She wouldn't be much good packing fuel.

The lark in its bright cage filled the wheelhouse with gay twittering. Wilder wished it would shut up.

The afternoon passed slowly and Wilder convinced himself that his fears were nonsense. Cathy had been upset the first day she'd mentioned Swatow; she must since have recognized the absurdity of the plan. The expectation of her footsteps along the passageway kept him awake, and finally he gave up any effort to sleep. There was constant movement through the ship now; the *Chiku Shan* was becoming a floating woodpile. He heard the squealing of a pig. News came to him in bright flurries as the villagers returned from their various explorations. They had found a small village tucked behind an apron of farms, some five miles to the west. The village itself had been avoided, but one pig, nine chickens, and several catties of rice had been purchased from farmers in the fields. True, the prices were criminal, but one must eat. No, Cathy had not been with them. Perhaps she was out with the others, gathering wood.

That afternoon the new Han baby was born in one of the texas cabins.

Wilder listened to the strange new wail and watched the villagers, returning in twos and threes. Suddenly he hated the sight of them. He wanted to see the flash of blonde hair along the mud flat, but only Chinese faces came and went, grinning under their burdens.

She had been gone more than six hours.

"Secure that wood!" he shouted. "Lash it down! Let's not have it wash overboard at the first swell."

The cargo spaces had grown impassable with driftwood; it ought to be enough fuel to get them all the way to Hong Kong. Wilder kept on the move to keep from thinking. She'd be back. Give her time. He got one of the broken guy wires spliced and hooked up again, taking some of the strain off the hurricane deck. He stopped to pick up bits of news. If the Feng family expected to eat, the old man would have to pay generously with his gold. The family sat morosely under guard in a corner of the saloon and they couldn't avoid the cooking odors from the stove. They would no longer be considered guests and unfortunately seasickness had passed and hunger returned.

By five o'clock it was clear that Cathy wasn't coming back.

Wilder despised the ticking of the clock on the bulkhead. A great hollowness settled inside him. He gazed at the battlement of cliffs rising outside the pilothouse windows. He could almost reach out and pull weeds from the soil of Red China. She was out there somewhere. Alone.

The little idiot! He gazed savagely at his taped and swollen ankle. But the thought of continuing the voyage without Cathy was a finer torture. Well, how far would he get with a bum leg? She was a little idiot and he loved her with a new and bewildering incandescence. The *Chiku Shan* ought to pull out with the first night tide that would float them off the mud, but there was no room in his mind for that.

He swung away from the window. All right, how far

had she got? This had been her last chance to get off the ferry within spitting distance of Swatow, and she'd taken it. If she could make the north road and stay out of trouble, she might reach Swatow that night. She was fool enough to believe her father was alive, and that was that. Well, what the hell did she think she could do alone even if he were?

And he wasn't. Wilder remained convinced of it. All she could hope to do was slap the face of the nearest commissar, but maybe that was enough. It would be a splendid gesture and a grand suicide. All right, he thought miserably, that was the way she was made.

The ship began to creak as the incoming tide lapped across the mud. Wilder lowered himself down the ladder. He supposed there'd be water enough under them to move out by seven or eight o'clock, but it no longer seemed important. Had Cathy headed for that village for directions? She was British and that wasn't yet a crime in Red China.

He collared one of the villagers who'd gone with the food-gathering expedition that morning. He got directions. You hit a path once you got beyond the stand of cypress. He hesitated before leaving the ship and climbed the ladder again to roll the chief engineer out of his bunk.

"You might as well start making steam. You might want it tonight."

Tack got his bloodshot eyes open and found the stub of a cigarette to light. "There is plenty of time. The boiler cools slowly. You fall asleep at the wheel, eh, Captain?" He grinned and pinched the skin of his face as if to loosen it. "She could drive a truck, that girl."

"I'm taking off. If I don't get back—good luck."

"You joke."

"Listen to me."

"Like this it happened." Tack seemed unaware of

what Wilder had said. "We get you out of the way and she say she can steer. Me, I'm too tired to care. O.K., baby, you steer. But we go slow, sticking poles in the water, plenty rocks in the way, you understand. All right. Miss Grainger make very cool pilot, I tell you, Captain. Then we come to deep water. When sun come up we're off beach. Move along rocks, find this spot, fit us like a glove. Beginner luck, eh?"

Wilder turned away uneasily. "She's gone."

"What?"

"She's convinced her father is alive in Swatow."

"Crazy."

"Then she's gone off to spit in some commissar's eye."

Wilder left the ship. He worked his way forward, the mud sucking at his legs. Stragglers, their backs loaded high with driftwood, were returning one by one. Wilder found his way up the cliffside and stopped to catch his breath. His leg was hurting again. He looked down at the *Chiku Shan*, its paddle wheel floating in a shallow mirror that hadn't yet reached the bow. She looked like an old rag-picker of a ship down there and she looked beautiful. He turned away. The sun was behind the cage of trees and he started toward it.

After ten minutes it was desperation alone that kept him going. He had stopped thinking. He knew that if he let himself think he'd turn back. The sun set and he found the worn ruts of an abandoned dirt road. He loped along, dimly aware that it was utter madness. She might have picked up a ride. She might already be walking the streets of Swatow.

The stars came down one by one to mock him. He stumbled and fell and lay there rubbing his leg. He picked himself up and wiped the grit off his lips and tried to hurry.

An hour after dark he was suddenly aware that something was on the move ahead of him on the road. Fatigue had washed out his sense of caution and he kept going.

Was that a glint of Cathy's blonde hair? His eyes tightened against the darkness and he knew it was only some trick of his mind. He rubbed his eyes and tried to find it again.

It was there. It was a woman. The starlight suddenly etched in the details as they drew closer.

It was Cathy.

Her hair was fallen, the dust of Chinese soil lay across her cheeks, but it was Cathy.

They stopped a few feet from each other on the lonely ruts.

"Tom!"

"Cathy, baby!"

They fell into a violent embrace. The touch of her skin was fire to his fingertips. He felt her quick tears against his cheek, hot and eager and intimate. He kissed her hungrily.

"Darling," she sobbed. "I turned back. I couldn't … go on. I was terrified that you'd leave before—"

"Baby, baby, I couldn't have left you."

"Darling, I need you. I need you desperately."

"I love you, Cathy. Do you understand? I love you."

Her fingers dug into his back. "Keep saying that. For years and years."

Chapter Twenty-five

The *Chiku Shan* spent almost an hour raiding the fishing stakes within a mile of Tongmi Point. Stars floated in the broad teacup of the bay. The great shadow of Mount Simpson stood to the west, and, some fifteen miles away, the Chilang Point beacon probed the night.

The bag nets were pulled up and stolen fish silvered the bow. The ferryboat had reached Hiechechin, the first of four gaping bays that stood between them and Hong Kong. Mount Simpson rose like the first of a rank of old friends pointing the way to Victoria Peak. To Wilder there was something fresh and buoyant in the air. The taxis, the double-decked streetcars, the rattling cable cars stood a hundred miles away. He could hear them in his mind.

He thought they must have taken a ton of fish aboard and made a signal to knock off below. He rang for slow speed, felt his way through the fishing stakes, and stood out of the bay.

Despite her protests, Cathy had been put to bed, and Koxinga quickly found his way back to the bathtub. She had returned to the ship in something close to shock and exhaustion. During the last mile or two of her trek back she had fallen into sobs. She had been sure Wilder and the *Chiku Shan* would be gone when she reached the cliffs.

With its main deck piled high with wood, the ferry rode low in the water and steered sluggishly. Wilder decided to put the Chilang Point light well behind them before he shot sparks out of the funnel.

The sound of Cathy's voice stayed with him in the pilothouse. She had tamed herself that day, he thought; she had returned to the ship a woman and she loved him with a woman's passion. To Wilder the world had suddenly turned itself inside out, and maybe it wasn't such a bad place. Love had appeared unexpectedly, like finding a genie in a bottle, but he had no desire now to cork the bottle. He loved Cathy. It was a brilliant, burnished thing inside him. It was the first bit of magnificence that had ever come into his life and he was going to hold onto it.

The hours at the wheel passed in flashes of recognition. With the whitewashed rock off Chilang Point behind them he passed to the south of Reef Islets and the vaulting night shape of Goat Island. The land streak to starboard fell back and he knew they were crossing the forty-mile maw of Honghai Bay. He glanced at the clock. It was just past three o'clock. They could never reach the far shore of the bay before daylight, but there were scrappy little islands sticking up in the bay to hide in.

Whale Rock popped into his mind, but he couldn't remember whether or not it was awash. He wished again he had a decent chart to plan by. What about Honghai Island itself? With the *Chiku Shan's* flat bottom, they could get over the foul ground and have the place to themselves.

An hour later he noticed that the barometer had begun to fall again, and this time he was willing to believe it.

They stayed in the shelter of Honghai Island for two days. Rain fell with tropical fury and splendor. Winds came and went, driving surf against the painted tadpole eyes of the ship and racking her wooden spine. They had the bay to themselves and the island bulk shielded them from shore, several choppy miles off. Rice vanished again from their menu and they ate fish. They waited, content to be sheltered from the weather, but anxious for it to break. Hong Kong lay some sixty miles away. Wilder kept lookouts posted on the island, but the weather had swept the bay of junks. Shoal waters stretched for better than a mile seaward of the island.

Wilder's leg began to heal and Cathy had changed.

She was given to silences now, and every time she looked at him it was a declaration of love. It was not a bad two days, and she was entirely beautiful.

Old Feng held out in his cabin, despite the hungry notes sent up by his family, until the morning of the second day. Finally his own ravenous stomach spoke and his greasy cache began to change hands. A single fish cost him its weight in gold. He signed receipts and the other Fengs were freely fed. The village would be far from insolvent when it reached Hong Kong.

Sometime during the second night the winds faded and died out, leaving only the hissing downpour. By noon Wilder decided to risk the obscurity of the afternoon. It might rain for a week. They could be in Hong Kong by morning. When they were less than a quarter of a mile out of Honghai Island a five-inch shell exploded a rock to port, raining fragments across the decks.

Wilder pushed Cathy away from the window.

"Get down!"

The gunboat had been patiently sitting in deep water, ready to blow the *Chiku Shan* apart the moment she left the island shoulder.

Chapter Twenty-six

Wilder raced the wheel and the bow strained around with exasperating laziness. He rang for full speed and got on the voice pipe.

"Chief engineer! Give us everything you've got! Blow us up if you have to, but get us out of here!"

"Aye, Captain, you bet!"

The thrashing stern had slipped around before the next shell came shrieking through the rain. Wilder didn't waste time trying to see the gunboat. It had obviously been waiting like a cat licking its chops, behind the curtain of rain, ready to pounce on the mouse trapped on its radar screen. Wilder's only hope was to keep in shoal waters, where the gunboat couldn't follow.

"Down there! Get at the bows with your goddamned poles!"

Water began to rush under the *Chiku Shan's* flat bottom, and the machined heartbeat of the ship quickened. The ferry picked up new vibrations and shook as if she were coming down with an attack of fever. Almost at once the rattle of twenty-millimeter guns came chattering through the downpour.

"Tom—"

"Better grab the wheel."

He left the helm before she reached it. The DE must be saving its five-inchers, he thought, until they could make a barn-door target out of the *Chiku Shan*. Ack-ack guns opened up. He glanced aft and pink bursts of fire flickered through the sheet of rain. Not more than two miles off, he thought.

He got to his chart and wood shattered below—the saloon.

"Zag it!"

"I am!"

He glanced desperately at his chart and the distant *pow! pow! pow!* reached the ferry. What had he remembered of Honghai Bay? Ross Head, an inlet he couldn't name, Fokai Point at the southwest tip of the bay. Not enough. He had to get past the point if he was going to get out of the bay at all. If he could slip into Bias Bay, below, he'd be able to play a nice game of tag through the islands. Well, they'd be driftwood before they saw Bias Bay unless he could get on a wide shelf of shallow water.

There were the coast shallows.

All right. He'd try going in. He'd try following the shoreline and hope to hell the gunboat couldn't get close enough to improve its marksmanship.

Wilder took the wheel and ordered Cathy to the deck. A moment later a stream of machine-gun fire rang off the tall black chimney just behind the pilothouse. Wilder cut the wheel and saw a rock awash out of the port window.

"I can see them, Tom!"

"I told you to get down!"

"They're cutting across behind us!"

Trying for the paddle wheel, he thought. He swung the wheel hard and ack-ack broke into the texas deck. Wood splintered and glass sang through the air. A rushing of feet broke out below.

Wilder kept bucketing toward shore at full speed while the DE dropped back in the danger of two- and three-fathom water. A mile or two off, Wilder could see the streaked hilly shoreline ahead and hoped they weren't beginning to panic below. He doubted whether there was a fathom of water under them now, and they were far from licked. They had a flat belly and the DE didn't.

"Can you still see them behind us?"

"Darling, they're falling back!"

"You're damned right they are!"

He finally straightened out and steered so close to shore that their sparks almost fell on land. He knew they were still caged on the DE's radarscope, but the five-inch gunnery had been less than expert; if the ferry could keep itself out of visual range the smaller guns might do only random damage.

"Chief engineer!"

"You are going to beach us, Captain!"

"Vary your speed. Let's not give their gunnery officer a chance to plot our positions. Keep our speed erratic.

Do you understand?"

The gunboat let go with a blind fury of firepower. A five-incher sucked air across the pilothouse windows, exploding in the cliffs to starboard and showering the ferry with wet sod. There were screams from wounded below, and Cathy left the wheelhouse. Lead began chewing up metal behind Wilder's back. The funnel again—it would be a sieve. The shallow water was keeping the gunboat at an enraged arm's length, but the shells kept flying. A moment later the saloon took a hit and the after end of the hurricane deck collapsed. A brass kettle went spinning over the bow like an absurd duck. Wilder knew there must have been villagers killed on the spot. Had Cathy gone back there?

He kept his eyes on the rain-pocked waters ahead. If he put the *Chiku Shan* on a sand bar or submerged rock she'd be a sitting target and that would be the end of her. The villagers kept working their bamboo poles and making arm signals to guide him. Gradually the distant firepower trailed off and finally there was only the hearty chunking of the paddle wheel. The cliffs fell away and Wilder saw several junks anchored in a shallow bight. The coolies appeared to have taken off for the hills.

The gunboat's silence became a strain. What the hell were they up to now? Wilder asked himself. Where had Cathy gone?

They thrashed along the lower rim of the bay, moving closer to Hong Kong with every mile, but it was no comfort.

Big Han climbed up to the pilothouse, and Wilder asked, "Have you seen Cathy?"

"No. We have taken bad damage. Many want to jump overboard. Land is so close."

"Don't let them. See if Cathy is all right."

"Yes, *ch'uan-chang*."

It was only after Big Han had left that Wilder realized he had put on the iron apron his grandfather had worn during the days of Koxinga.

The gunboat wasn't making a sound.

Wilder thought he had it figured out. She must be exploring with her fathometer for some position ahead along the shoreline, a depth closer in where she could stop the *Chiku Shan* cold.

The ferry churned past an inlet, marked with buoys and swollen with rain, and Wilder was tempted to turn into it. But he had no idea if it went anywhere and he might only be bottling them up. There was nothing to do but keep going and hope the shallows held all the way around Fokai Point.

A moment later Big Han returned with a grin, his iron apron clanking, and he didn't have to say it. Cathy was safe, and Wilder could take a breath.

The DE seemed to have vanished. The *Chiku Shan* hugged the coast in silence for better than two hours. Tensions relaxed and Wilder saw an occasional grin below. Did they think it was over? The paddle wheel thrashed under the glowering sentinel of Harlem Peak, dimly seen through the rain, and then the shore fell away to the long sandy isthmus that led to the knobby rocks of Fokai Point. They had passed a narrow river emptying into the bay and Wilder found himself tightening up at the wheel again. The point couldn't be more than six or seven miles ahead, and he knew the gunboat had no intention of letting the Chiku Shan out of the bay.

They hit incoming swells and the tall funnel began to draw smoky figures in the air.

"Chief engineer!"

"Aye, Captain! We knock off for lunch, eh?"

"How much wood have you?"

"Perhaps we steam another five hours."

"We'd better."

A shadow appeared through the wet windows and Wilder found himself looking broadside at a steel-jacketed monster. The gunboat had found a chink in the shallows.

"Full speed *astern!* The bastard's dead ahead of us!"

The *Chiku Shan* crawled over her own boiling wake and one of the gun turrets let go. The five-incher dropped short, raising a muddy gusher just off the bow. Wilder welcomed the incoming swells now, for they tipped the DE's aim, and he felt a new respect for the *Chiku Shan's* narrow beam. Dead on, she was a high, skinny target. The heavy machine guns opened up again, clanging like a shooting gallery against the capstan, and the other five-incher sent its shock through the downpour. The shell screamed high. The machine guns climbed and windows began to explode. Wilder ducked. They backtracked fast while the gunboat stood in its chink and its captain no doubt raged at his gunners. Wilder kept the ferry at reverse to protect the paddle wheel from direct fire. He remembered passing a river minutes before and decided to try for it.

The DE left its chink, slipping back under the rain, and its guns lost their visual target in the rain. There wasn't a window left in the pilothouse and Wilder steered with one hand on the wheel and searched the shore. The mouth of the river came drifting toward them. Once past it, he began swinging the wheel.

"Full speed ahead!"

The *Chiku Shan* took a swell on its beam. The bows turned into the river and the paddle wheel churned foam into the bay. Glancing behind, Wilder saw that the DE had pulled well out of its ambush; wet flashes were coming astern of them. But she damned well couldn't follow them into the river.

Wilder followed a bend that put a low sandy hill between them and the bay. The gunboat lobbed shells far and wide. The misshapen woodpile chunked along and Wilder felt some small glint of victory. The Red captain would probably be put to chipping paint for letting the turtle of a ferryboat get away. Well, the turtle of a ferryboat was where she belonged—on a river.

They bucketed in under the rising bulk of cliffs, streaked here and there with new waterfalls. On the port side rice paddies began to appear, flooded over their dikes. A mile out of the bay a whiteness stood ahead of them on the river and the surface boiled with froth and crabs' eyes. Wilder reached for the bell cord.

Rapids.

Flat bottom or not, they couldn't climb rapids. They were stopped. Wilder posted two machine gunners at the stern and sent the other two to find positions around the bend, and he was sorry if they were going to get soaked. The five-inch guns were still breaking through with an occasional disheartened boom; the ferry must still be on the scope. If only he could have got her tucked well behind a radar shield of hills!

The captain would tire of wasting ammunition, Wilder thought, and a couple of boatloads of Red sailors would come upriver to put the ferry out of her misery.

It was past six when he left the pilothouse. It amazed him to see what a shambles he'd been dragging. The hog post was down in a tangle of wires. The funnel breathed smoke through a thousand pores. The hurricane deck had caved in on the blown-out after end of the saloon. The kitchen had been wiped out and the rain washed splinters and blood along the weather decks. There were eleven dead.

Cathy was busy with the wounded and ignored him except for a hurried glance.

"Let's clean up this ship!" Wilder shouted angrily. "Get up! You think we're going to come steaming into Hong Kong looking like a junk heap? *Tsou-k'uai!* Loose wood can be stacked for the furnace, cousins! We're not forty miles from safety!"

Wilder kept glancing at the wet sky and the rice fields to port.

There was still a chance.

At nine o'clock the machine guns at the bend opened up. It was a rattling half hour. Two whaleboats of Reds came upriver on their waspish engines to board the ferry, but only one of them got past the bend. Wilder was already at the stern when tommy-gun fire began to rake the ship.

"Blow the bastards out of the river," Wilder growled.

The *Chiku Shan's* two ancient machine guns began to cough on their tripods. He heard the coxswain's bell jingle as it took a spray of lead. Wilder didn't wait to see the end of it. He got hold of Big Han.

"Get your paint and your brushes."

"Yes, *ch'uan-chang*."

"I want you to draw a patrol boat and two whaleboats on the pilothouse bulkhead. The brightest colors you've got."

The flood across the rice field was rising.

They picked up seven survivors anxious to desert for Hong Kong.

At four in the morning Wilder rolled Tack out of his bunk.

"We're leaving."

"Aye, Captain. We have grown stilts to walk over the rapids."

"I'll give you five minutes to get at your Johnson bar, or I'll wrap it around your neck."

"My neck, Captain, could bend a Johnson bar."

"Did you have your men keep steam in the boiler?"

"I ordered it."

"I'll have the after end of the hurricane deck hacked up for firewood. It's not good for anything else now."

The ship came suddenly awake as the paddle wheel thumped over and started thrashing. Wilder had sent one of the villagers wading out over the rice fields and he returned muddy to the hips. There was enough flood water out there to float a battleship.

Wilder turned the bows to port and men probing the bottom with poles began to shout up the depths. "Two *ch'ih!* Two *ch'ih*, six *fen!* Three *ch'ih!* Three *ch'ih!*"

There was a wooden groan as they scraped over the riverbank and floated out over the submerged rice field. Wilder kept the engine throbbing at slow speed, feeling his way through the hissing dark. He edged along, putting the cliffs more solidly between the ferry and the DE to jam the radar. The decks below had come alive with curious heads. Had their captain cracked his brains?

The rice shoots brushed along the *Chiku Shan's* flat bottom.

"Two *ch'ih!* One *ch'ih*, eight *fen!* One *ch'ih*, seven *fen!*"

They slipped over the flooded dike and onto the next paddy. There was water to spare.

Finally Wilder put the ship south.

The rain lifted and the ferry seemed to shake itself off. The bulkheads dripped with small tinkling sounds. They passed the drenched roofs of a pagoda on a small hill, an island now, and visibility improved. Suddenly the depths increased beyond the length of their poles and Wilder assumed they had stumbled into a lake.

Stars appeared, their faces washed, and soon Wilder could make out the rooftops of a village to the west. Junks and sampans clustered in the distance. Shortly after five Wilder thought he had found a river cutting south along the length of the peninsula. It would empty into either Honghai Bay or Bias Bay. A small fleet of fishing junks, their lanterns roving, were on the move ahead of him, and he followed very slowly. What they thought of the dark monster behind, breathing sparks, he couldn't guess, but he supposed fear kept driving them forward.

They led the *Chiku Shan* into Bias Bay, pink with dawn, and Wilder rang for full speed, scattering the junks as he churned down on them. He glanced behind at the hills obscuring Fokai Point and hoped the DE thought it still had the ferryboat up the creek. Perhaps its captain was kicking the radar to make it tell the truth. Even a turtle of a ferryboat can't vanish in the shallowness of a lake stream.

Before the ship had dried itself in the sun Wilder found Pedro Blanco Island, which he had never been able to place in his mind. It came up in the distance to port, like three white tree stumps sitting on the horizon.

They burned everything they could lay hands on, including two carved and heavily lacquered coffins. Wilder had a cup of tea in one hand when he sighted Mirs Point to starboard.

"Powder your nose, baby." He grinned. "We're crossing the line into British waters."

She moved to the starboard window space and gazed rigidly at the final rocky corner of Red China. Wilder didn't try to guess what was going through her mind, but he knew she was willing to see the point pass behind them. The sun was brittle on the waters ahead of them. It was, Wilder decided, a hell of a fine morning, and Victoria Peak would be wearing white clouds, like an English magistrate sitting in judgment.

"I'll never go back, Tom," Cathy said softly.

Fine, he thought. Splendid.

Junks raised their square sterns across their path and the sunny hills and bays of the New Territories framed themselves in the broken windows. The moments quickened. They passed south of the Ninepin Group, like whales lazing in the morning, and finally Wilder nosed the *Chiku Shan* into the sparkling blue waters of Tathong Channel. He realized he was sweating and very possibly grinning his head off. Freighters and warships flying a dozen Western flags stood off his broken yellow jack staff and it was the finest sight that had ever met his eyes. He grabbed the whistle. He held onto it for the next hour, up past Junk Island to starboard and Hong Kong Island to port. The paddle wheel came thrashing around the bend, the whistle screaming in its faintly delirious little voice, and harbor traffic paused to gape.

It was the closest Wilder had ever felt to coming home.

The docks and prairie of rooftops that were Kowloon stretched out to their right and he could see a train huffing along the eastern shore. And there, on the left, the steep green backdrop with Hong Kong at its feet—Victoria. Wilder gazed at the tall brick chimneys, the docks and go-downs, the smart villas overhanging the city. He could see a cable car rattling up to the cloudy peak.

"Look, baby."

Cathy kissed his grinning cheeks. "We *did* make it, darling!"

"Maybe we don't look like the *Queen Mary*, but we *made* it. And look at the peak. She's wearing her best wig for us."

"Do you suppose there's a joss-pidgin-man in Hong Kong?"

"There damned well better be."

"I love you, darling."

"It figures."

The stern buckets kicked up a proud bustle of spray and Wilder shrugged off an old humiliation. He felt cleansed. He had settled the score and more. He had found out what he was made of. He had got to Hong Kong on one leg and he could look the world squarely in the eye. He window-shopped as they passed the sights of Hong Kong and he felt as eager as a kid to grab Cathy's hand and get ashore. She was his. The world was his.

For the first time since the voyage had begun he saw Old Feng on deck. He appeared at the bow, a pumpkin shape under a straw hat, and maybe he was grinning too.

Wilder decided he would take the *Chiku Shan* around the island to Aberdeen Bay, jammed with its floating colonies of junks and sampans, and ground the ferry. And there it would stay. And they could put it on the map as Chiku Shan Island if they wanted to, a navigational danger of lacquer carvers, dollmakers, and fishermen.

"Let me take the whistle, darling. Please!"

"I love you, baby," he said.

"It figures."

Impulsively he turned the *Chiku Shan* toward Peddars Wharf and pulled in beside the bright paintwork of the Kowloon ferry, and the heart of Hong Kong spread out before them.

An astonished crowd was already forming.

THE END

A. S. Fleischman Bibliography
(1920-2010)

NOVELS
The Straw Donkey Case (1948)
Murder's No Accident (1949)
Shanghai Flame (1951)
Look Behind You, Lady (1952) [reprinted as *Chinese Crimson*, UK, 1962]
Danger in Paradise (1953)
Counterspy Express (1954)
Malay Woman (1954) [reprinted as *Malay Manhunt*, UK, 1966]
Blood Alley (1955)
Yellowleg (1960) [reprinted as *The Deadly Companions*, 1961]
The Venetian Blonde (1963)
The Sun Worshippers (2012)

SHORT STORIES
The Girl from Lavender Street (*Bluebook*, Feb 1954)

SCREENPLAYS
Blood Alley (1955)
Goodbye, My Lady [as Sid Fleischman] (1956)
Lafayette Escadrille (1958)
The Deadly Companions (1961)
Scalawag (1973)
The Whipping Boy [as Max Brindle] (1995)

As Sid Fleischman

FICTION
Mr. Mysterious & Company (1962)
By the Great Horn Spoon! (1963)
Ghost in the Noonday Sun (1965)
Chancy and the Grand Rascal (1966)
McBroom Tells the Truth (1966)
McBroom and the Big Wind (1967)
McBroom's Zoo (1969)
Longbeard the Wizard (1970)
Jingo Django (1971)
McBroom's Ear (1971)
McBroom's Ghost (1971)

The Wooden Cat Man (1972)
McBroom Tells a Lie (1976)
Kate's Secret Riddle Book (1977)
Me and the Man on the Moon-Eyed Horse (1977)
Humbug Mountain (1978)
Jim Bridger's Alarm Clock and Other Tall Tales (1978)
McBroom and the Beanstalk (1978)
The Hey Hey Man (1979)
McBroom and the Great Race (1980)
The Case of the Cackling Ghost (1981)
McBroom the Rainmaker (1982)
McBroom's Almanac (1984)
Whipping Boy (1986)
The Scarebird (1987)
The Midnight Horse (1990)
Jim Ugly (1992)
McBroom's Wonderful One-Acre Farm (1992)
The 13th Floor: A Ghost Story (1995)
The Abracadabra Kid: A Writer's Life (1996)
Bandit's Moon (1998)
The Ghost on Saturday Night (1999)
Here Comes McBroom!: Three More Tall Tales (1999)
A Carnival of Animals (2000)
Bo & Mzzz Mad (2003)
Disappearing Act (2003)
The Giant Rat of Sumatra: or Pirates Galore (2005)
Escape! The Story of the Great Houdini (2006)
The White Elephant (2006)
The Entertainer and the Dyybuk (2007)
The Trouble Begins at 8: A Life of Mark Twain in the Wild, Wild West (2008)
The Dream Stealer (2009)
Sir Charlie: Chaplin, the Funniest Man in the World (2010)

BOOKS ON MAGIC
Between Cocktails (1939)
Ready, Aim, Magic! (with Bob Gunther, 1942)
Call the Witness (with Bob Gunther, 1943)
The Blue Bug (with Bob Gunther, 1947)
Top Secrets (with Bob Gunther, 1947)
Magic Made Easy (as Carl March, 1953)
Mr. Mysterious's Secrets of Magic (1975)
The Charlatan's Handbook (1993)

Sid Fleischman, born Albert Sidney Fleischman in Brooklyn March 16, 1920, was no newcomer to adventure and mystery when he first began to write as A. S. Fleischman in the late 1940's. He began his professional life as a vaudeville magician and adventured around the Far East in the U.S. Navy during World War II. A novelist, screenwriter and playwright, he is also notable as a Newbery Medal winning author of children's books. Fleischman lived in Santa Monica, California, and passed away there on March 17, 2010.

Black Gat Books is a new line of mass market paperbacks introduced in 2015 by Stark House Press. New titles appear every other month, featuring the best in crime fiction reprints. Each book is size to 4.25" x 7", just like they used to be, and priced at $9.99 (1-31) and $10.99 (32-). Collect them all.

#	Title	Author	ISBN
1	Haven for the Damned	Harry Whittington	978-1-933586-75-5
2	Eddie's World	Charlie Stella	978-1-933586-76-2
3	Stranger at Home	Leigh Brackett	978-1-933586-78-6
4	The Persian Cat	John Flagg	978-1-933586-90-8
5	Only the Wicked	Gary Phillips	978-1-933586-93-9
6	Felony Tank	Malcolm Braly	978-1-933586-91-5
7	The Girl on the Bestseller List	Vin Packer	978-1-933586-98-4
8	She Got What She Wanted	Orrie Hitt	978-1-944520-04-5
9	The Woman on the Roof	Helen Nielsen	978-1-944520-13-7
10	Angel's Flight	Lou Cameron	978-1-944520-18-2
11	The Affair of Lady Westcott's	Gary Lovisi	978-1-944520-22-9
12	The Last Notch	Arnold Hano	978-1-944520-31-1
13	Never Say No to a Killer	Clifton Adams	978-1-944520-36-6
14	The Men from the Boys	Ed Lacy	978-1-944520-46-5
15	Frenzy of Evil	Henry Kane	978-1-944520-53-3
16	You'll Get Yours	William Ard	978-1-944520-54-0
17	End of the Line	Dolores & Bert Hitchens	978-1-944520-57-1
18	Frantic	Noël Calef	978-1-944520-66-3
19	The Hoods Take Over	Ovid Demaris	978-1-944520-73-1
20	Madball	Fredric Brown	978-1-944520-74-8
21	Stool Pigeon	Louis Malley	978-1-944520-81-6
22	The Living End	Frank Kane	978-1-944520-81-6
23	My Old Man's Badge	Ferguson Findley	978-1-944520-87-8
24	Tears Are For Angels	Paul Connelly	978-1-944520-92-2
25	Two Names for Death	E. P. Fenwick	978-1-951473-01-3
26	Dead Wrong	Lorenz Heller	978-1-951473-03-7
27	Little Sister	Robert Martin	978-1-951473-07-5
28	Satan Takes the Helm	Calvin Clements	978-1-951473-14-3
29	Cut Me In	Jack Karney	978-1-951473-18-1
30	Hoodlums	George Benet	978-1-951473-23-5
31	So Young, So Wicked	Jonathan Craig	978-1-951473-30-3
32	Tears of Jessie Hewett	Edna Sherry	978-1-951473-36-5
33	Repeat Performance	William O'Farrell	978-1-951473-42-6
34	The Girl With No Place to Hide	Marvin Albert	978-1-951473-49-5
35	Gang Rumble	Edward Aarons	978-1-951473-53-2
36	Back Country	William Fuller	978-1-951473-59-4
37	Killer	Robert Silverberg	978-1-951473-68-6

Stark House Press
1315 H Street, Eureka, CA 95501 (707) 498-3135
griffinskye3@sbcglobal.net www.starkhousepress.com
Available from your local bookstore or direct from the publisher

www.ingramcontent.com/pod-product-compliance
Lightning Source LLC
LaVergne TN
LVHW011937070526
838202LV00054B/4684